BABYMOUSE
GOES FOR THE GOLD

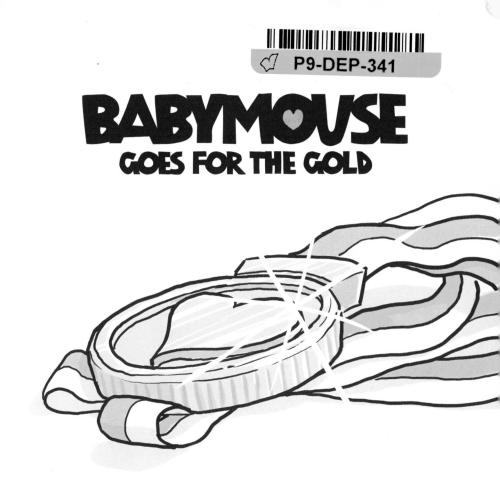

BY JENNIFER L. HOLM & MATTHEW HOLM

RANDOM HOUSE 🏠 NEW YORK

SPECIAL THANKS TO
JOEY WEISER AND MICHELE CHIDESTER
FOR COLORING ASSISTANCE!

All rights reserved. Published in the United States by Random House Children's Books, a division of Penguin Random House LLC, New York.

Random House and the colophon are registered trademarks of Penguin Random House LLC.

Visit us on the Web!
randomhousekids.com
Babymouse.com

Educators and librarians, for a variety of teaching tools, visit us at
RHTeachersLibrarians.com

Library of Congress Cataloging-in-Publication Data is available upon request.

ISBN 978-0-307-93163-4 (trade) — ISBN 978-0-375-97099-3 (lib. bdg.) —
ISBN 978-0-307-97546-1 (ebook)

MANUFACTURED IN MALAYSIA   10 9 8 7 6 5 4 3 2 1   First Edition

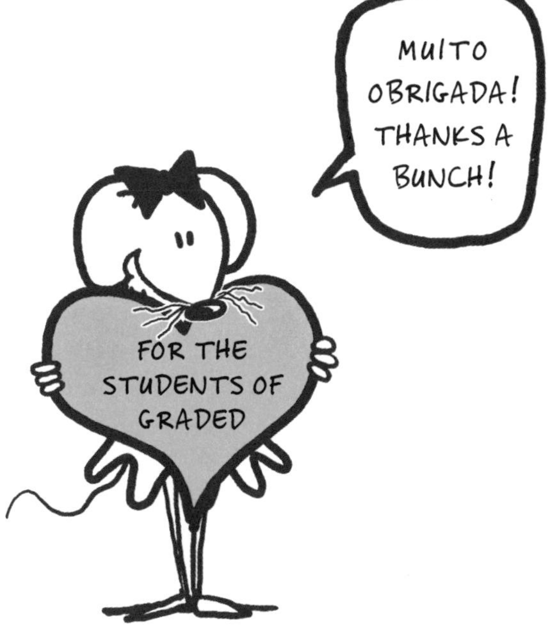
MUITO OBRIGADA! THANKS A BUNCH!
FOR THE STUDENTS OF GRADED

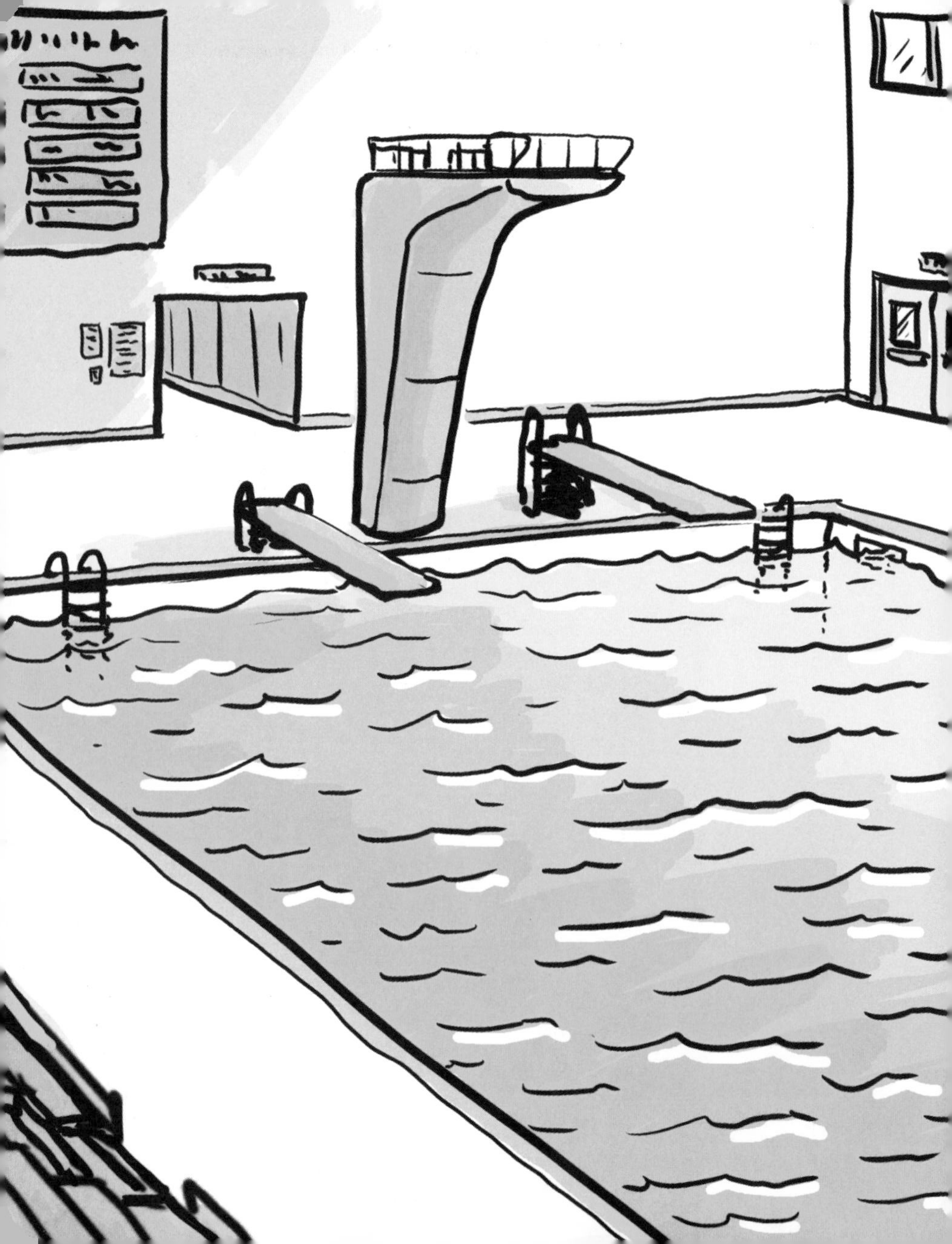

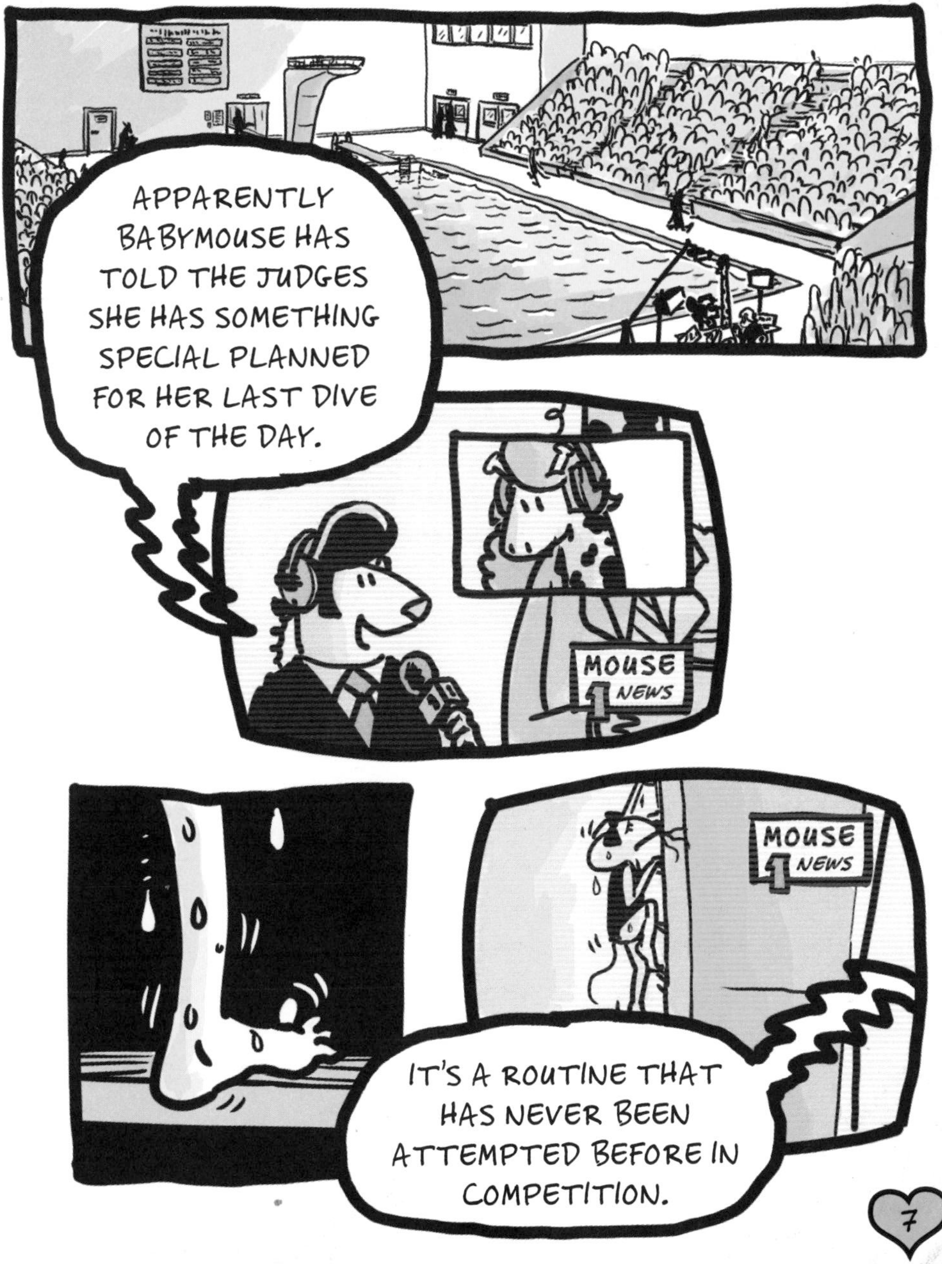
APPARENTLY BABYMOUSE HAS TOLD THE JUDGES SHE HAS SOMETHING SPECIAL PLANNED FOR HER LAST DIVE OF THE DAY.
MOUSE NEWS
MOUSE NEWS
IT'S A ROUTINE THAT HAS NEVER BEEN ATTEMPTED BEFORE IN COMPETITION.

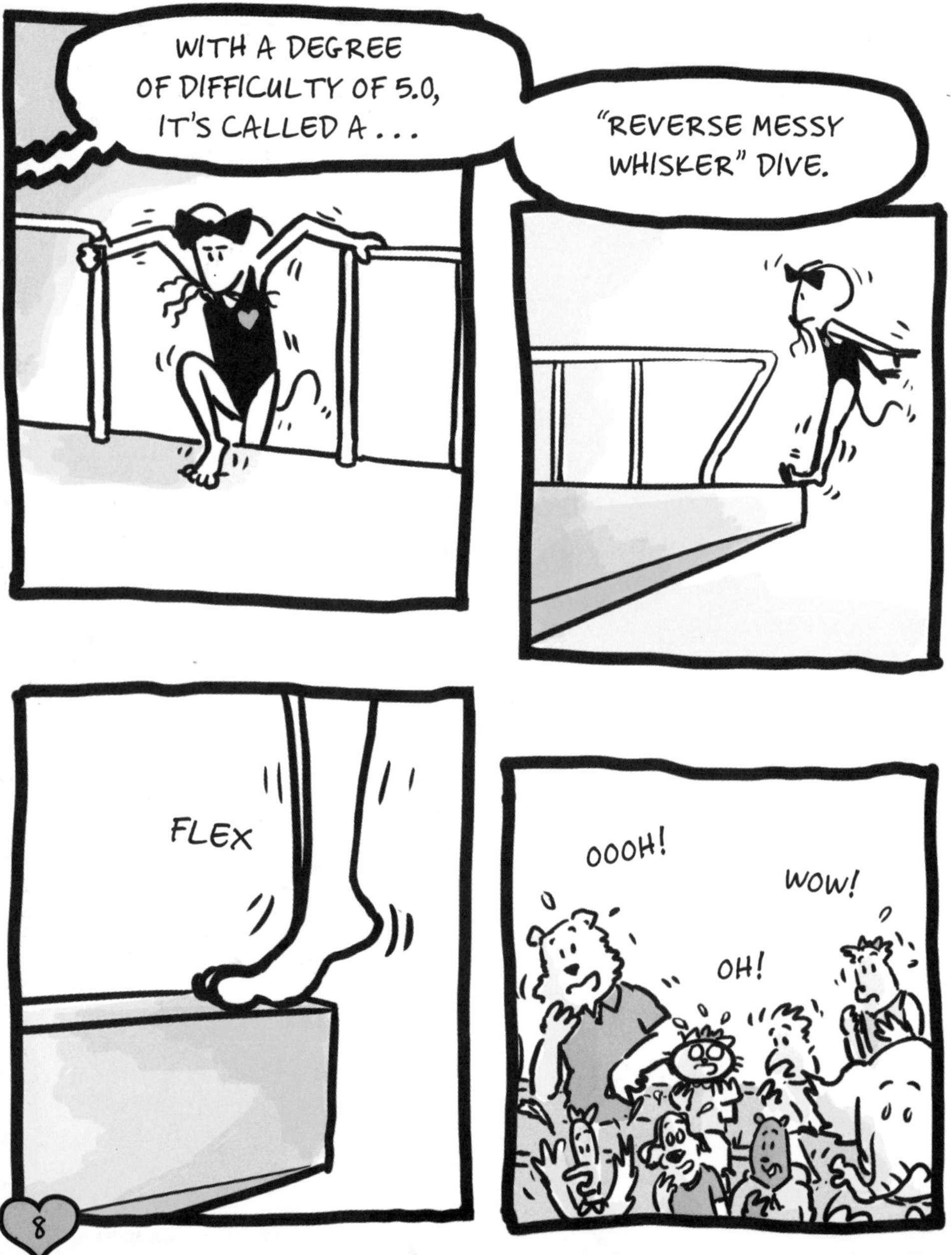
WITH A DEGREE OF DIFFICULTY OF 5.0, IT'S CALLED A . . .
"REVERSE MESSY WHISKER" DIVE.
FLEX
OOOH!
WOW!
OH!

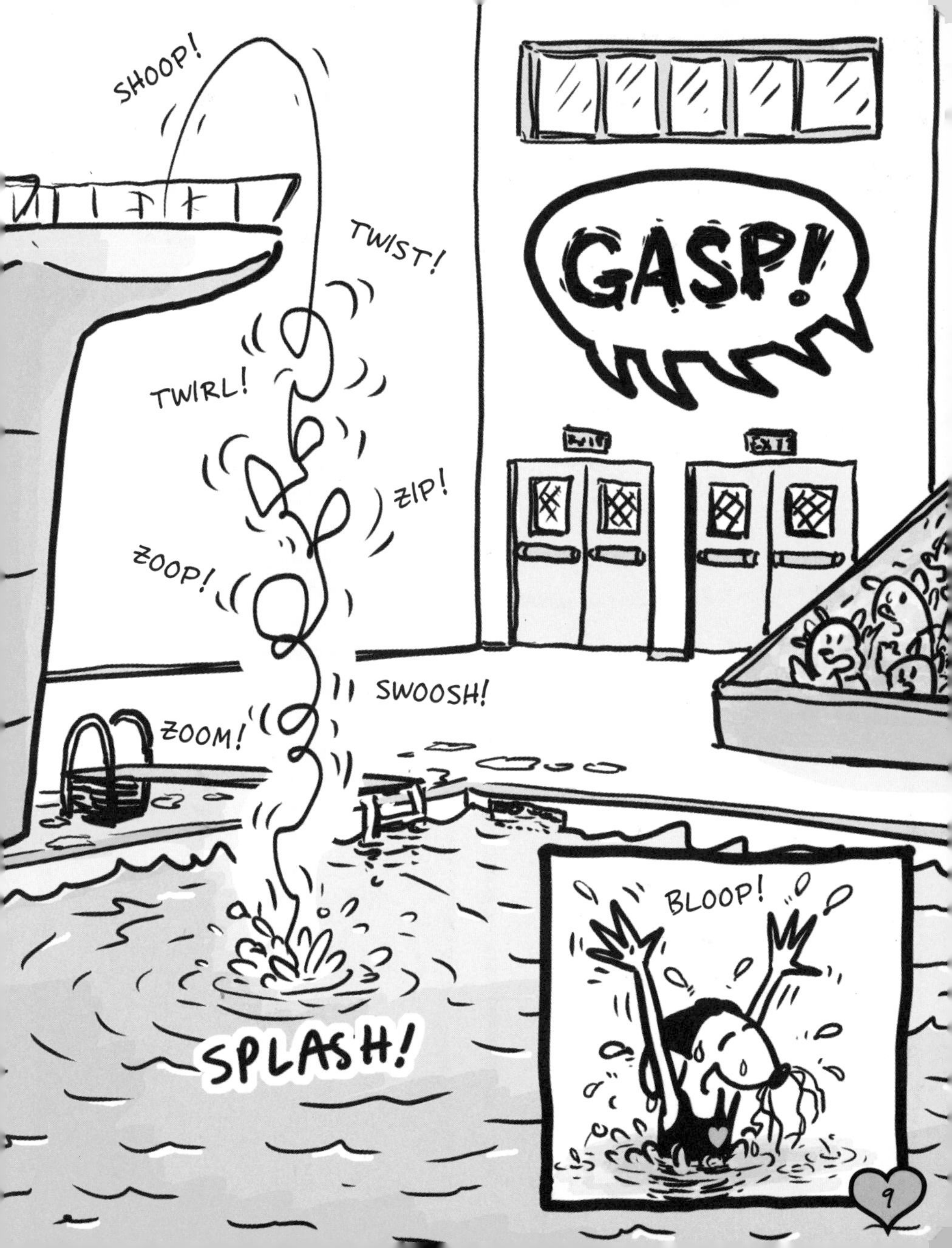
SHOOP!
TWIST!
TWIRL!
ZIP!
ZOOP!
SWOOSH!
ZOOM!
SPLASH!
GASP!
BLOOP!

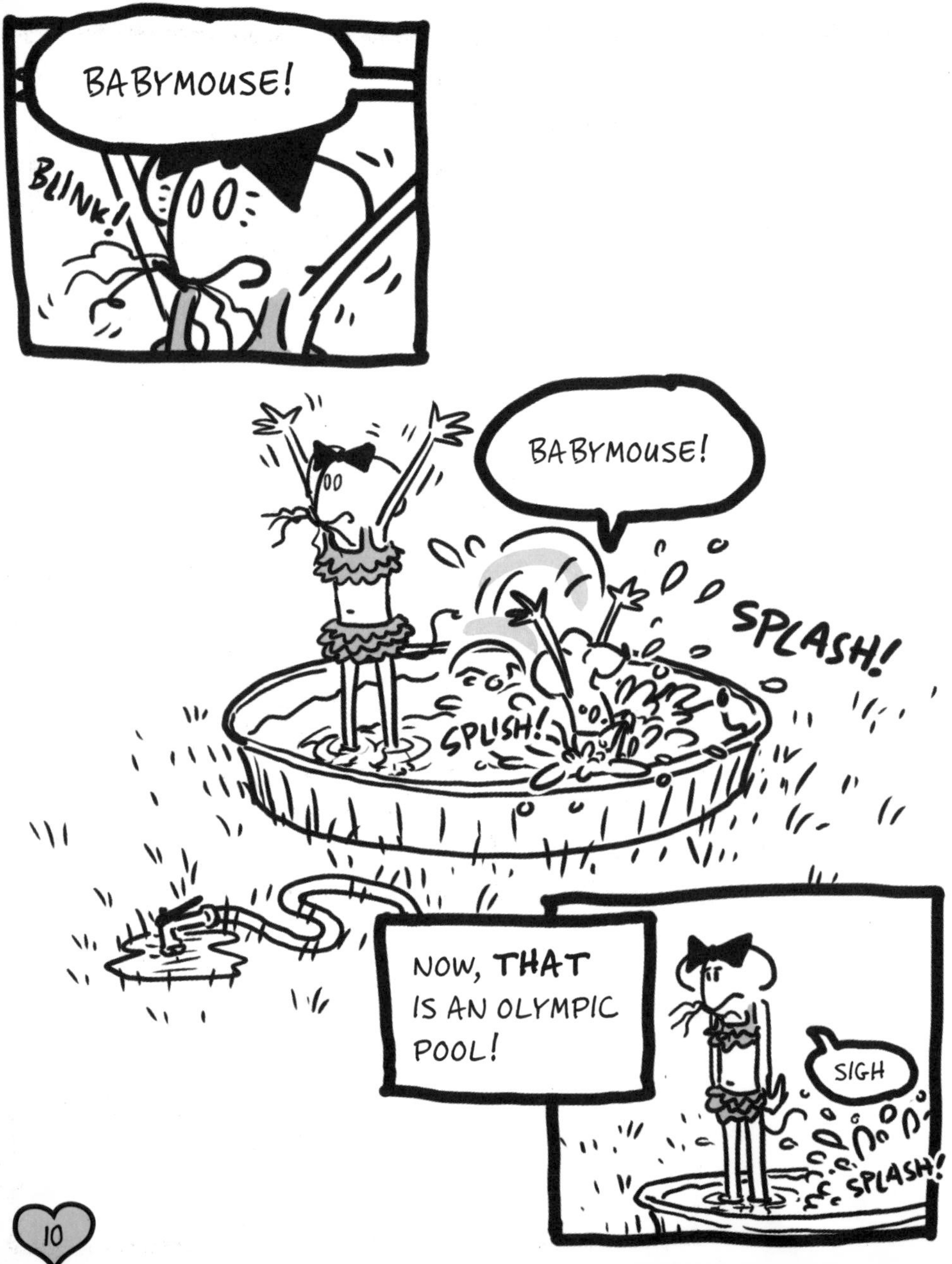
BABYMOUSE!
BLINK!
BABYMOUSE!
SPLASH!
SPLISH!
NOW, THAT IS AN OLYMPIC POOL!
SIGH
SPLASH!

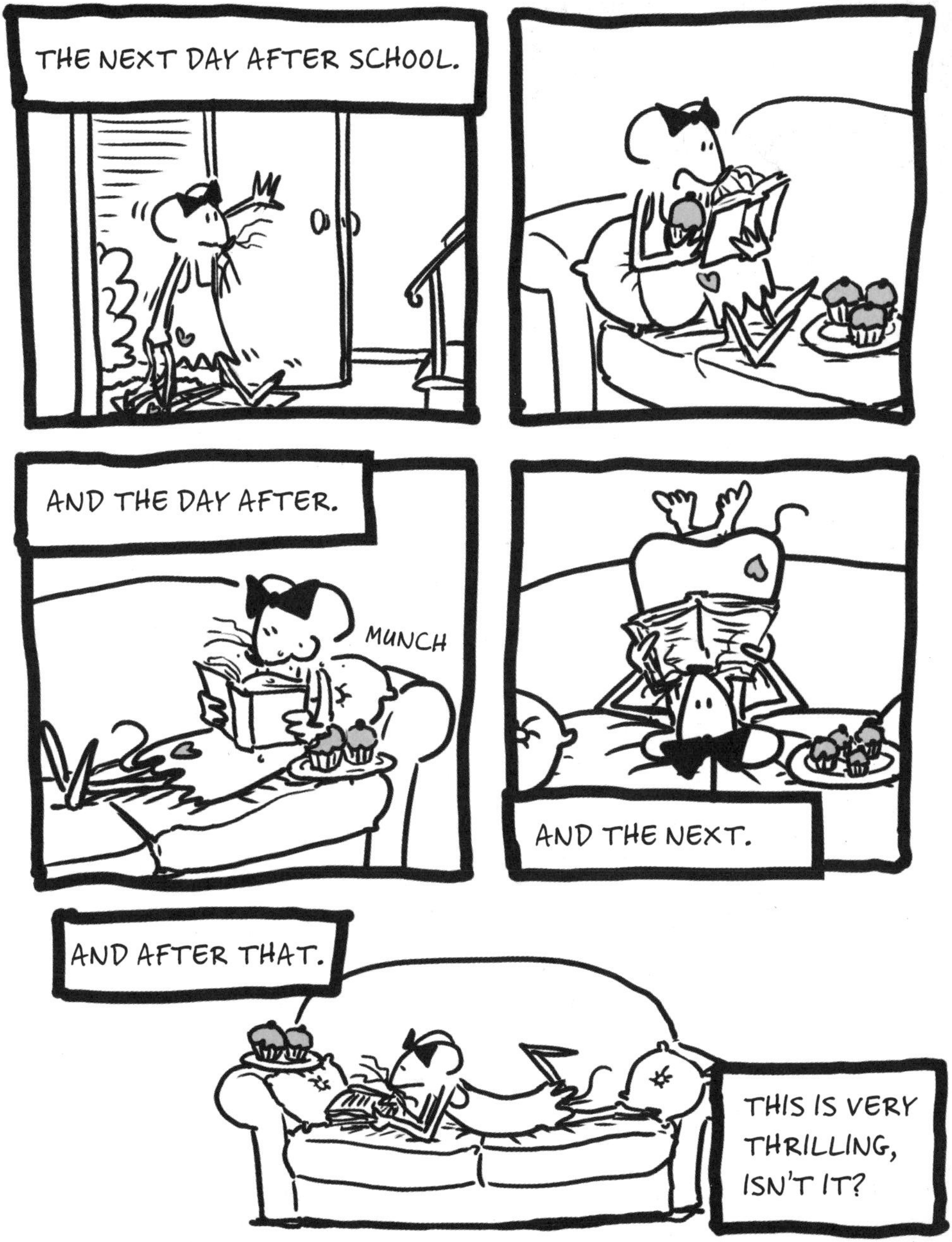
THE NEXT DAY AFTER SCHOOL.
AND THE DAY AFTER.
MUNCH
AND THE NEXT.
AND AFTER THAT.
THIS IS VERY THRILLING, ISN'T IT?

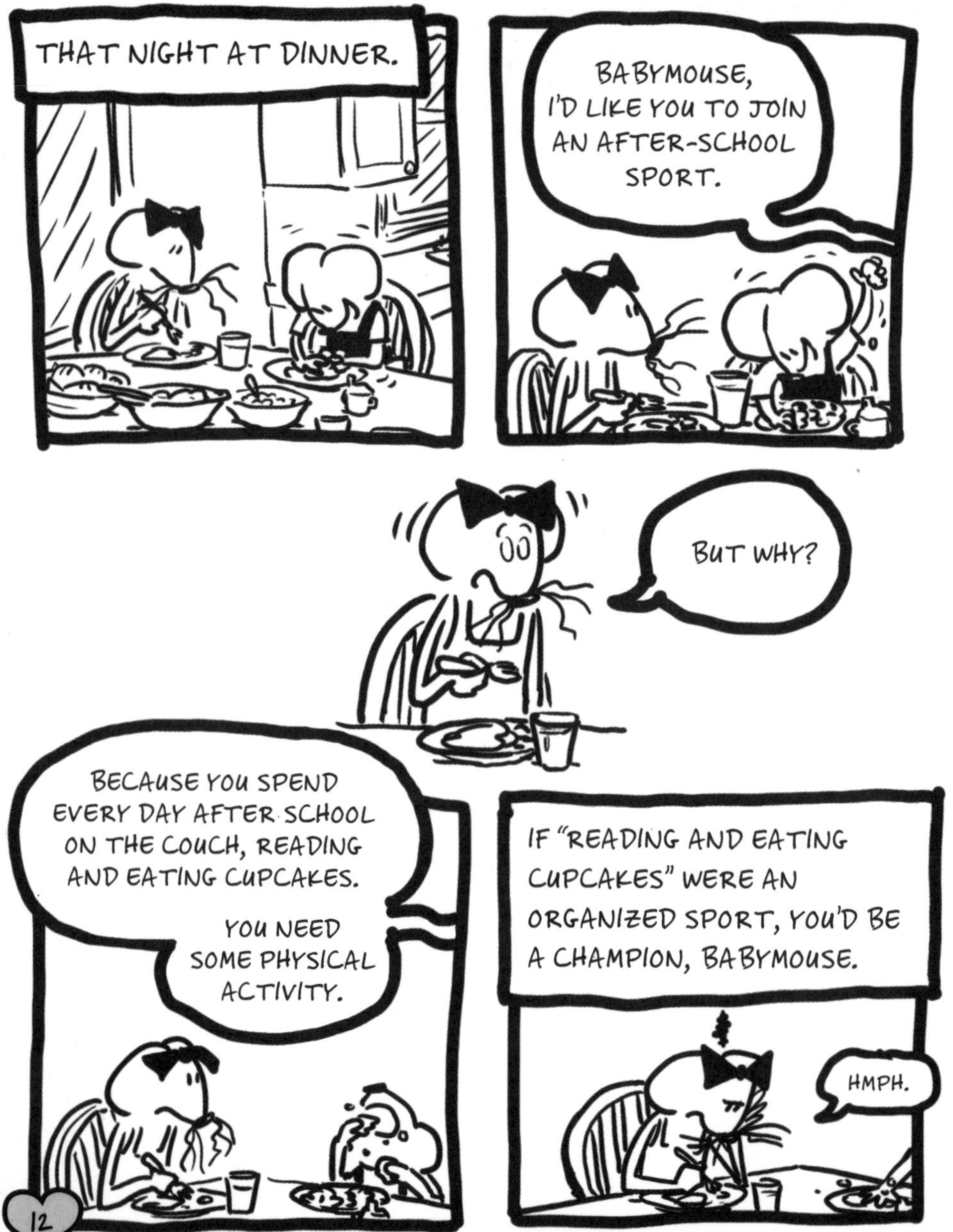
THAT NIGHT AT DINNER.
BABYMOUSE, I'D LIKE YOU TO JOIN AN AFTER-SCHOOL SPORT.
BUT WHY?
BECAUSE YOU SPEND EVERY DAY AFTER SCHOOL ON THE COUCH, READING AND EATING CUPCAKES.
YOU NEED SOME PHYSICAL ACTIVITY.
IF "READING AND EATING CUPCAKES" WERE AN ORGANIZED SPORT, YOU'D BE A CHAMPION, BABYMOUSE.
HMPH.

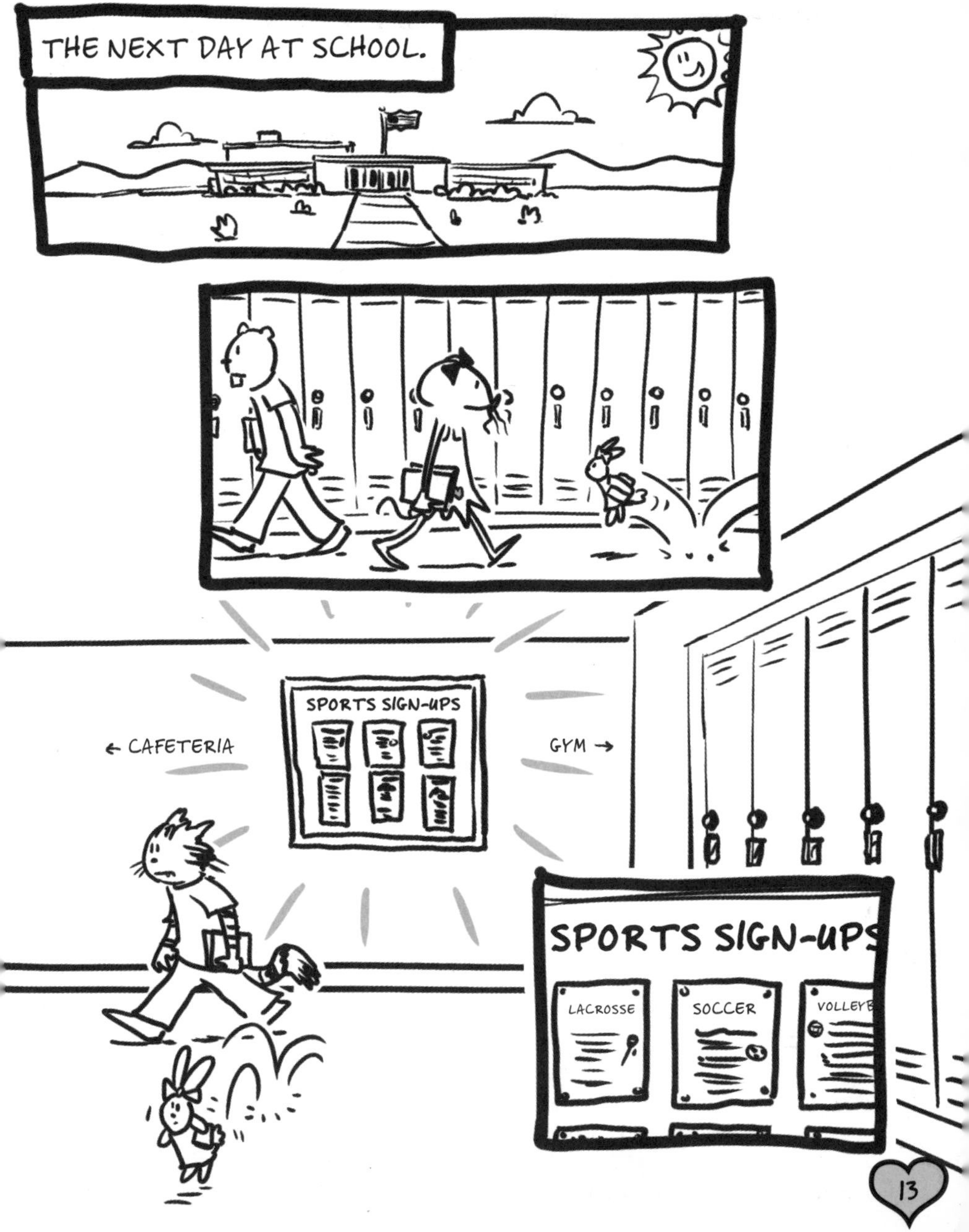
THE NEXT DAY AT SCHOOL.
SPORTS SIGN-UPS
← CAFETERIA
GYM →
SPORTS SIGN-UPS
LACROSSE
SOCCER

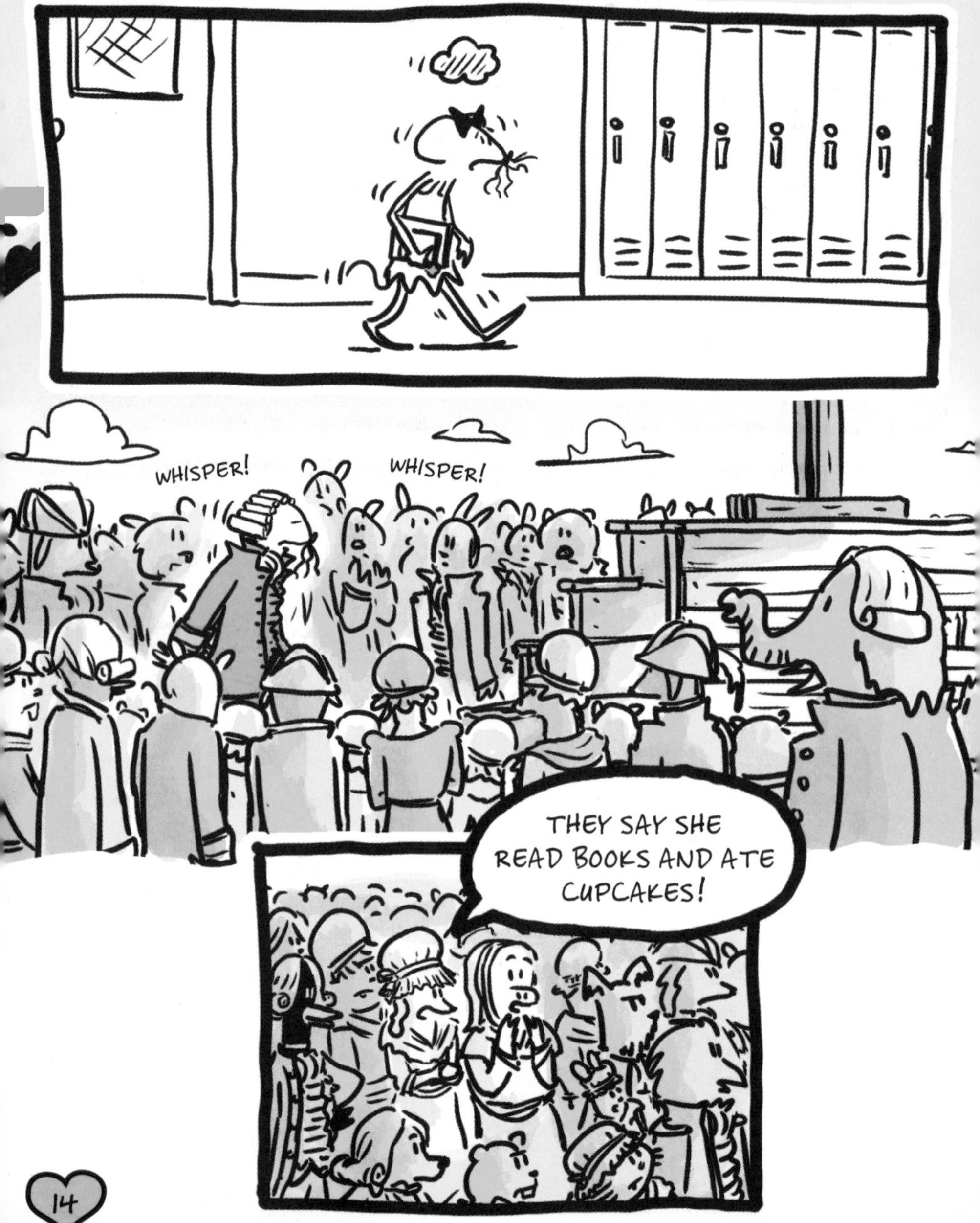
WHISPER!
WHISPER!
THEY SAY SHE READ BOOKS AND ATE CUPCAKES!

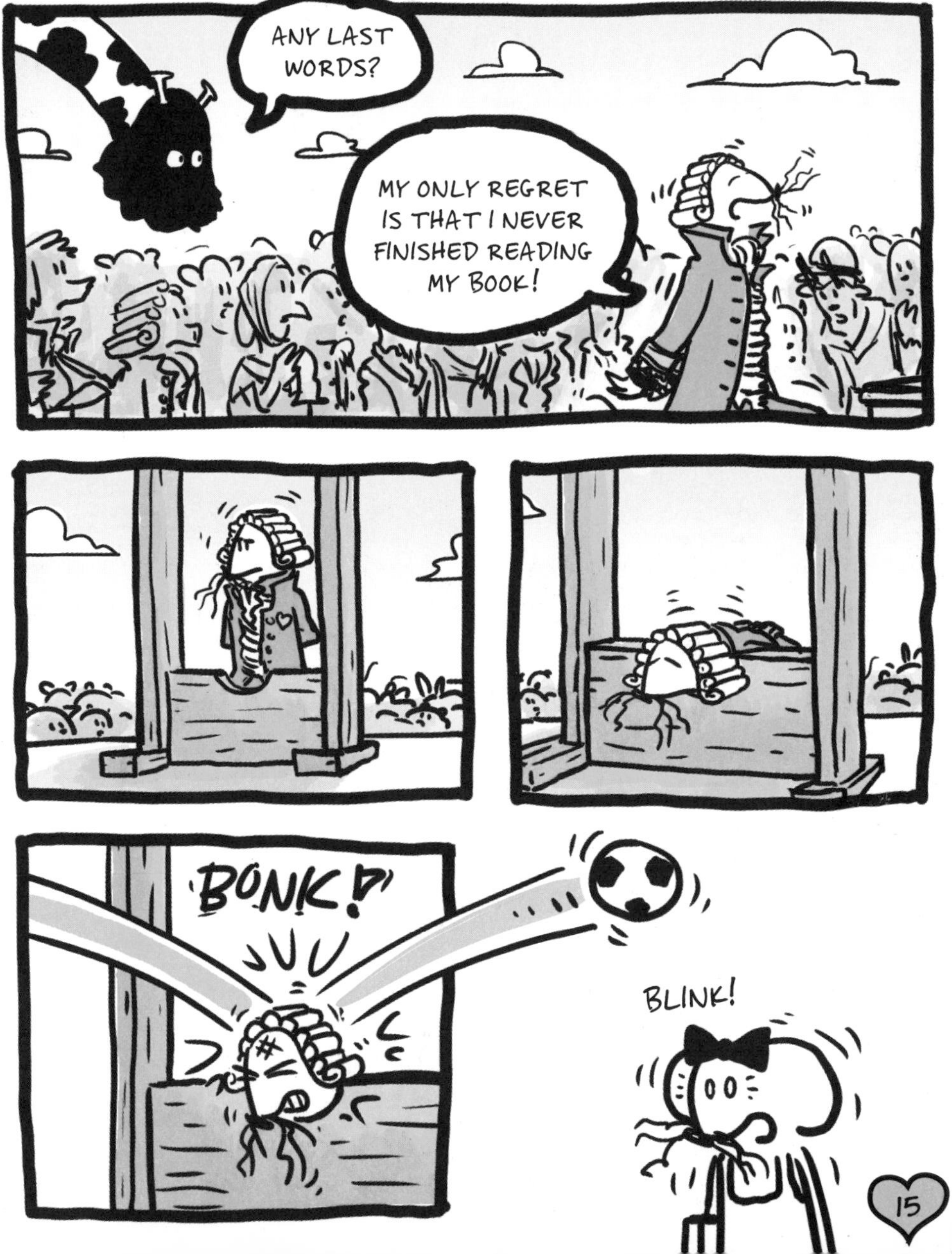
ANY LAST WORDS?
MY ONLY REGRET IS THAT I NEVER FINISHED READING MY BOOK!
BONK!
BLINK!

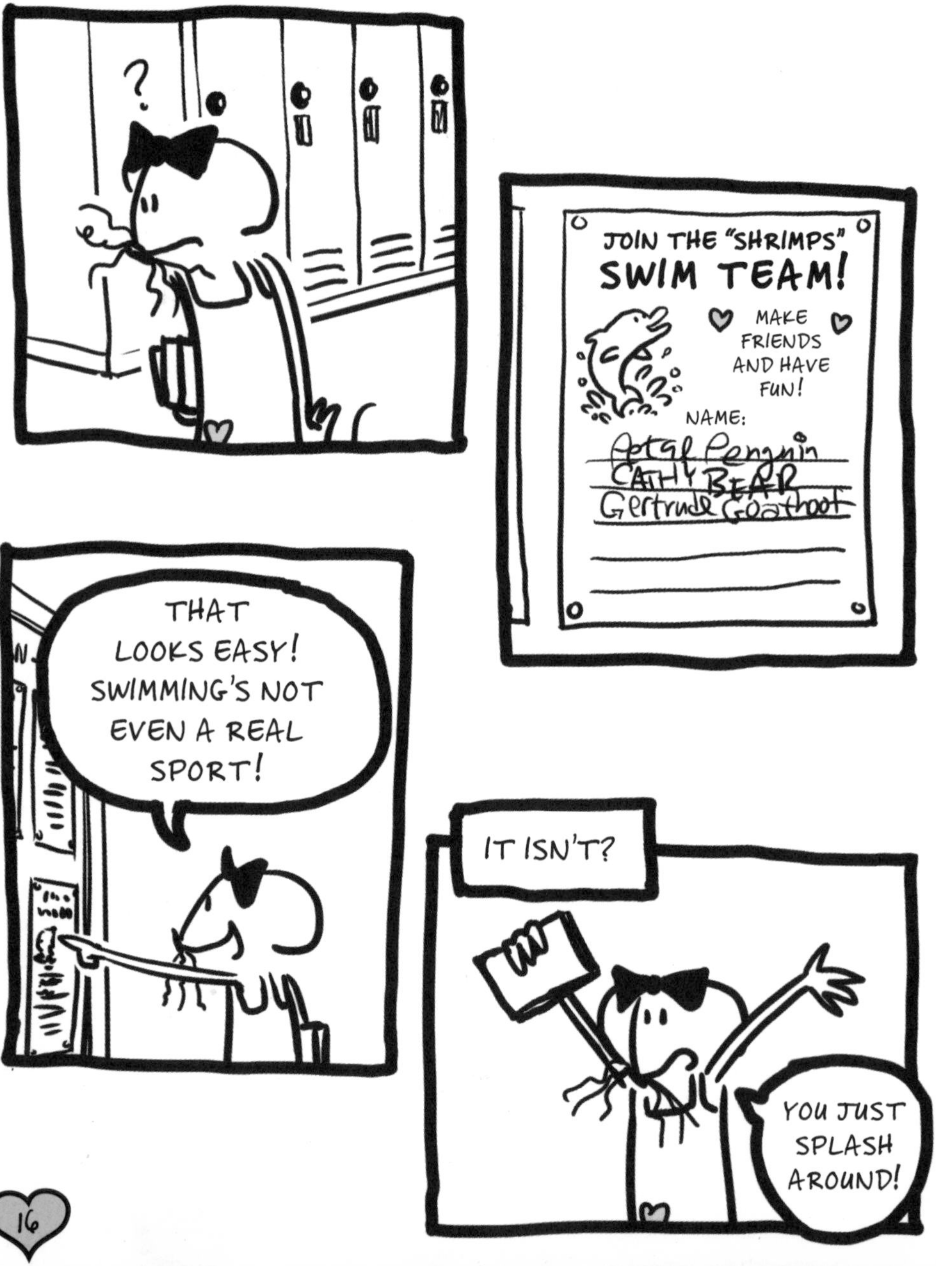
?
JOIN THE "SHRIMPS"
SWIM TEAM!
MAKE FRIENDS AND HAVE FUN!
NAME:
Cathy Bear
Gertrude Goathoof
THAT LOOKS EASY! SWIMMING'S NOT EVEN A REAL SPORT!
IT ISN'T?
YOU JUST SPLASH AROUND!

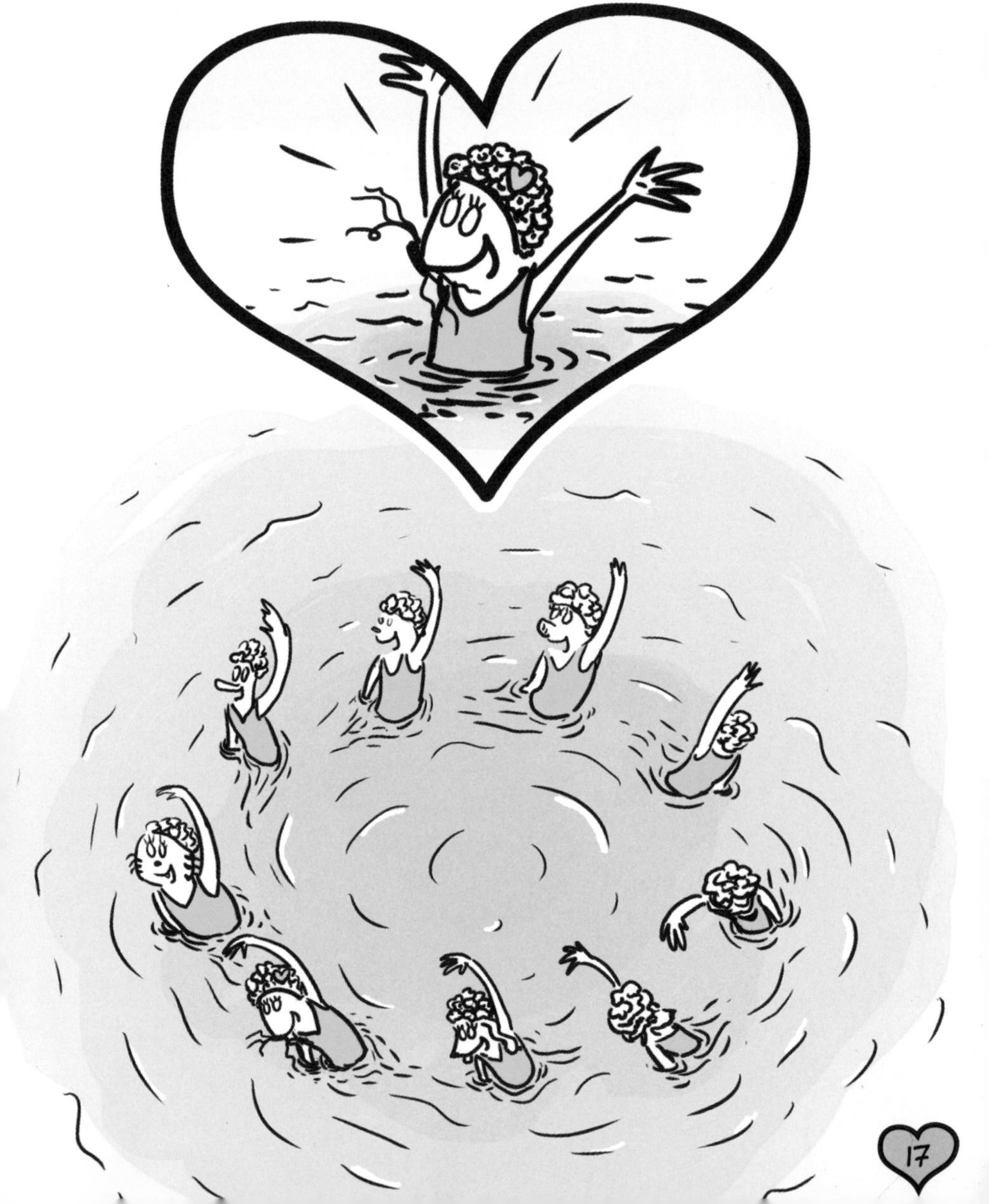

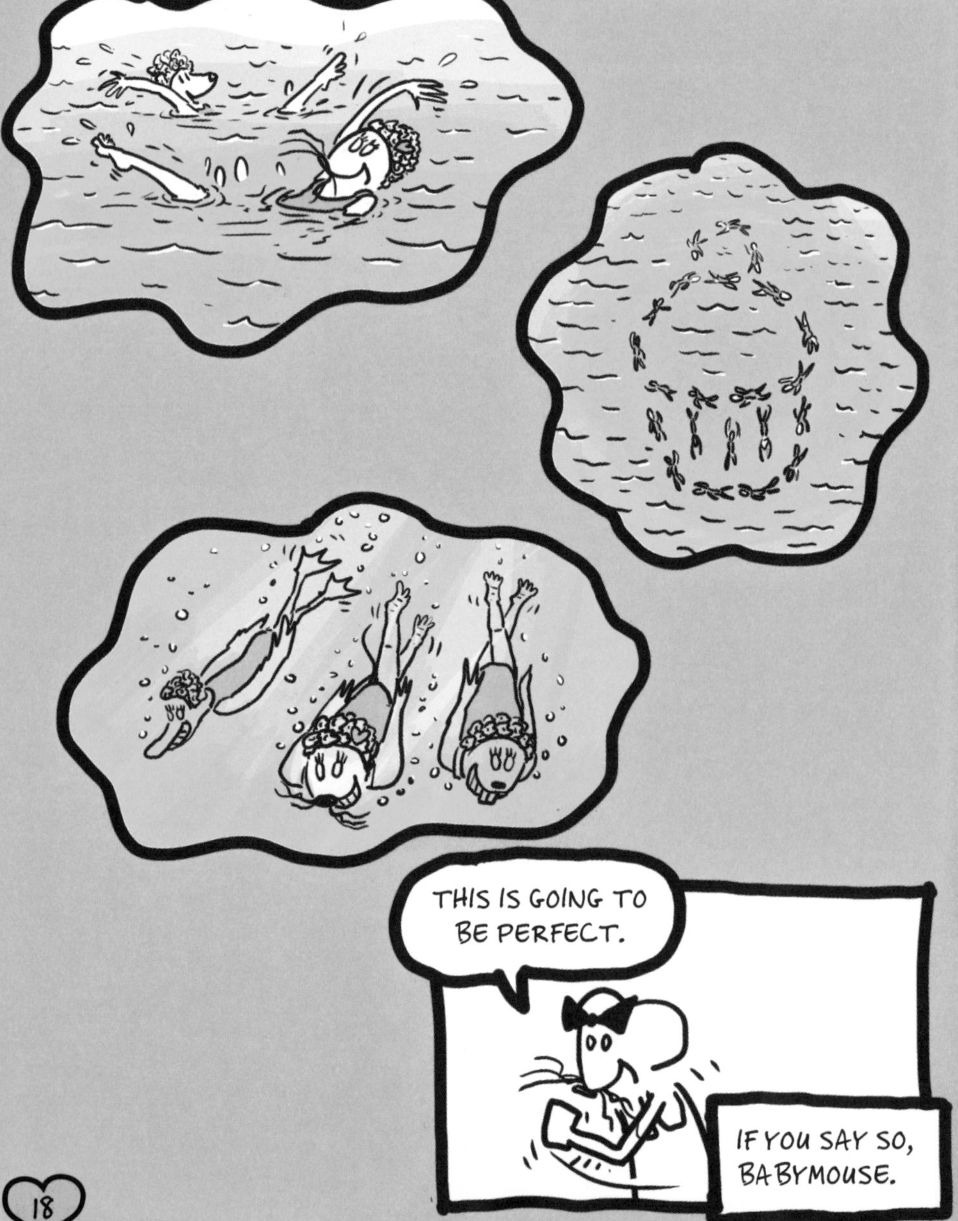
THIS IS GOING TO BE PERFECT.
IF YOU SAY SO, BABYMOUSE.

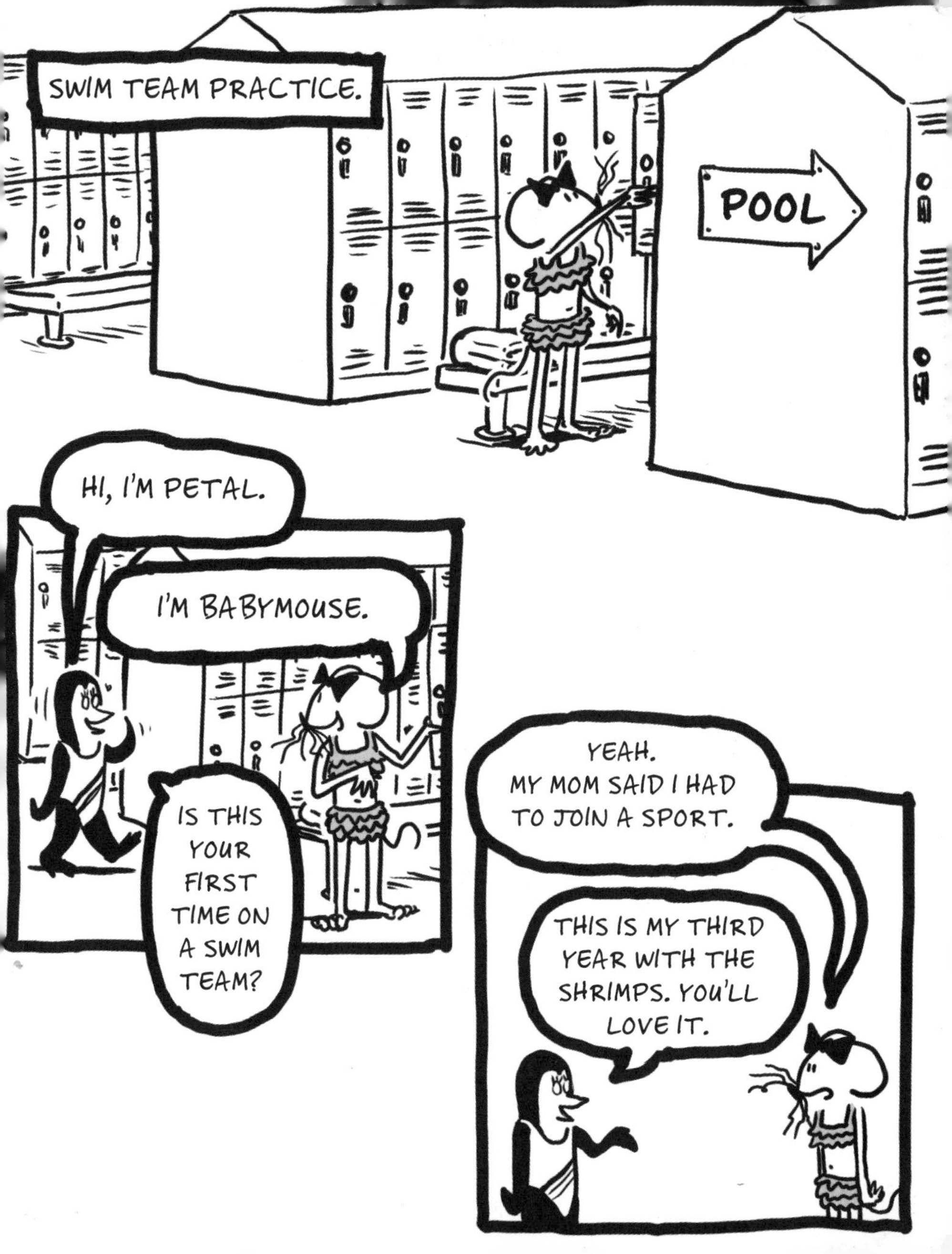
SWIM TEAM PRACTICE.
POOL
HI, I'M PETAL.
I'M BABYMOUSE.
IS THIS YOUR FIRST TIME ON A SWIM TEAM?
YEAH. MY MOM SAID I HAD TO JOIN A SPORT.
THIS IS MY THIRD YEAR WITH THE SHRIMPS. YOU'LL LOVE IT.

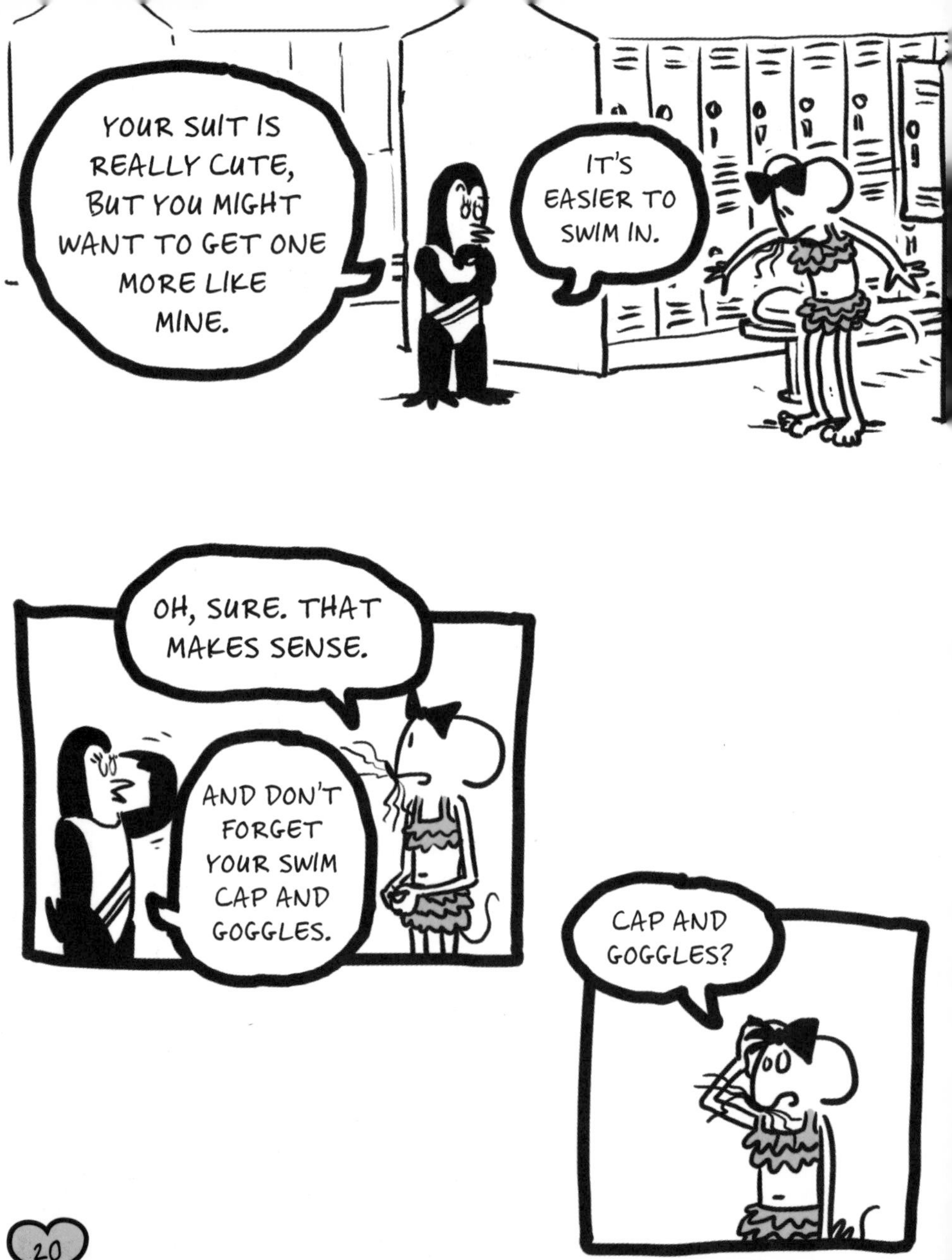
YOUR SUIT IS REALLY CUTE, BUT YOU MIGHT WANT TO GET ONE MORE LIKE MINE.
IT'S EASIER TO SWIM IN.
OH, SURE. THAT MAKES SENSE.
AND DON'T FORGET YOUR SWIM CAP AND GOGGLES.
CAP AND GOGGLES?

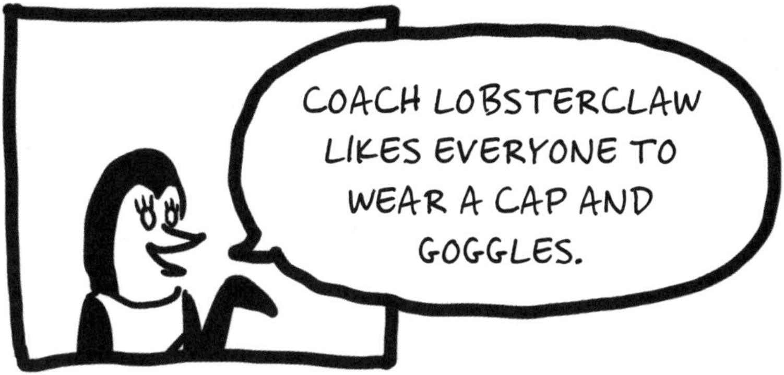
COACH LOBSTERCLAW LIKES EVERYONE TO WEAR A CAP AND GOGGLES.

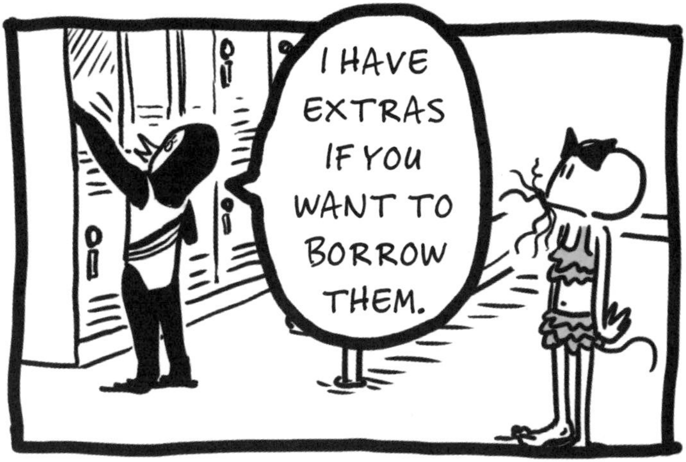
I HAVE EXTRAS IF YOU WANT TO BORROW THEM.

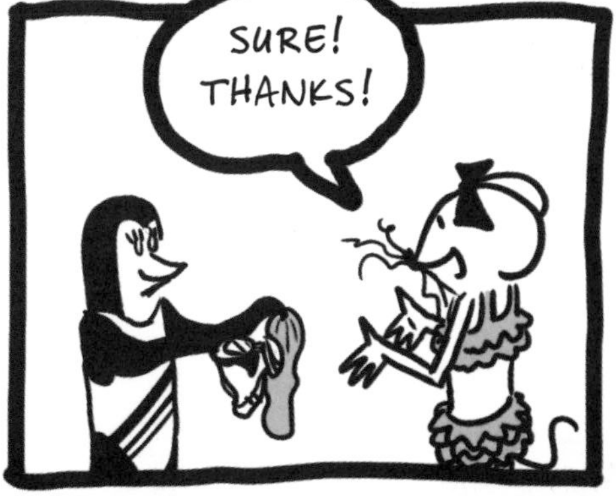
SURE! THANKS!

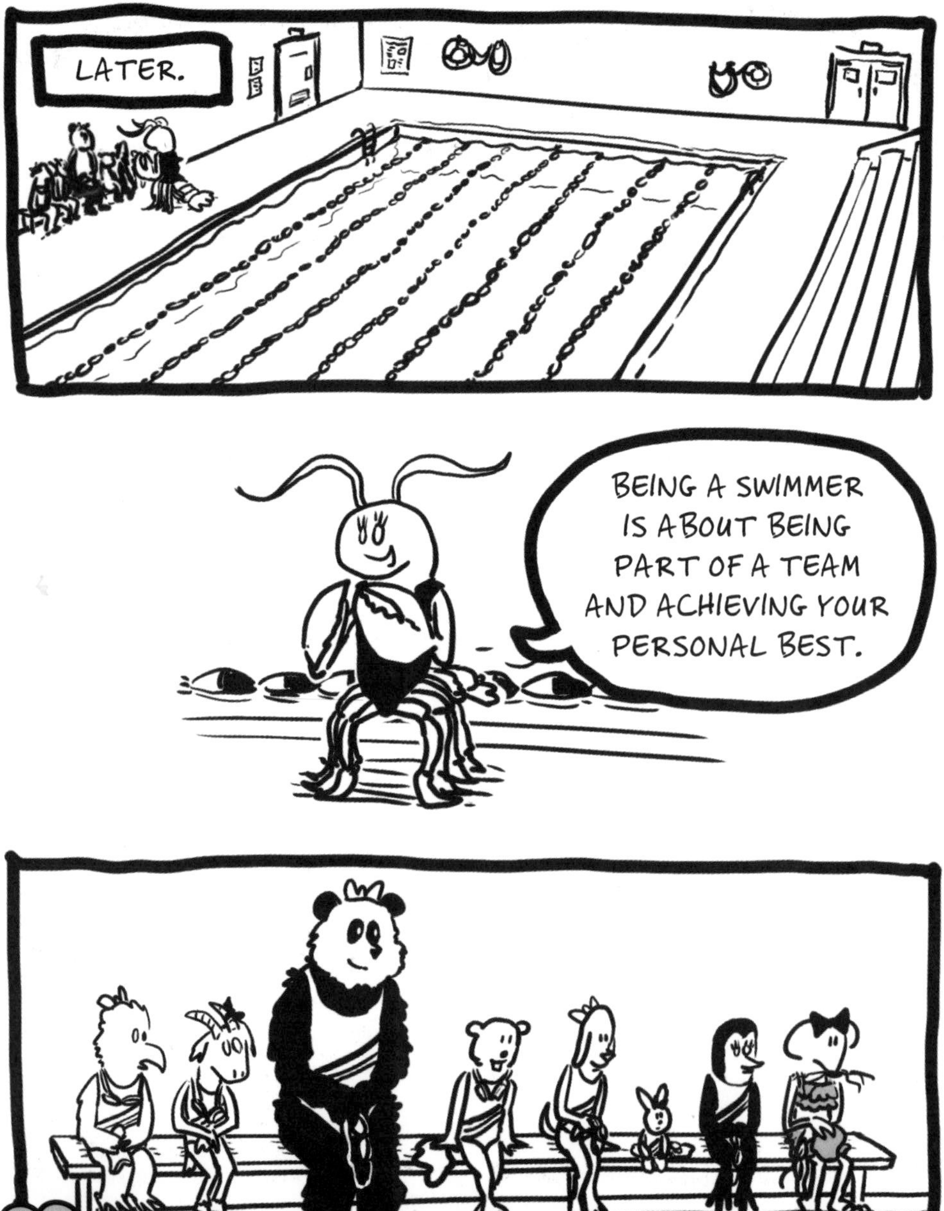
LATER.
BEING A SWIMMER IS ABOUT BEING PART OF A TEAM AND ACHIEVING YOUR PERSONAL BEST.

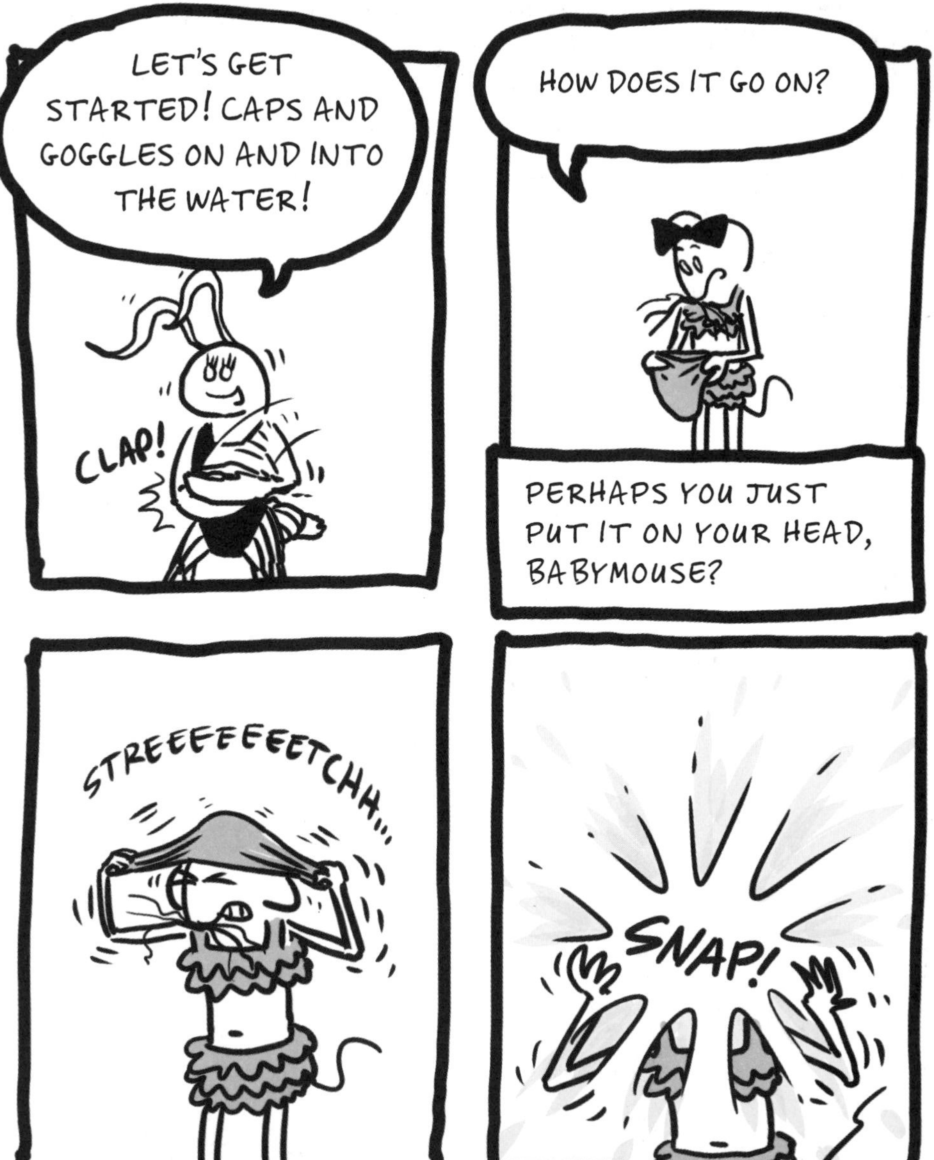
LET'S GET STARTED! CAPS AND GOGGLES ON AND INTO THE WATER!
CLAP!
HOW DOES IT GO ON?
PERHAPS YOU JUST PUT IT ON YOUR HEAD, BABYMOUSE?
STREEEEEEEETCHH...
SNAP!

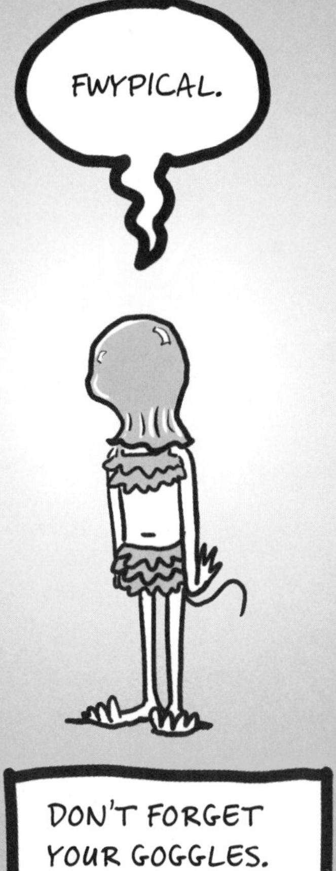
FWYPICAL.
DON'T FORGET YOUR GOGGLES.

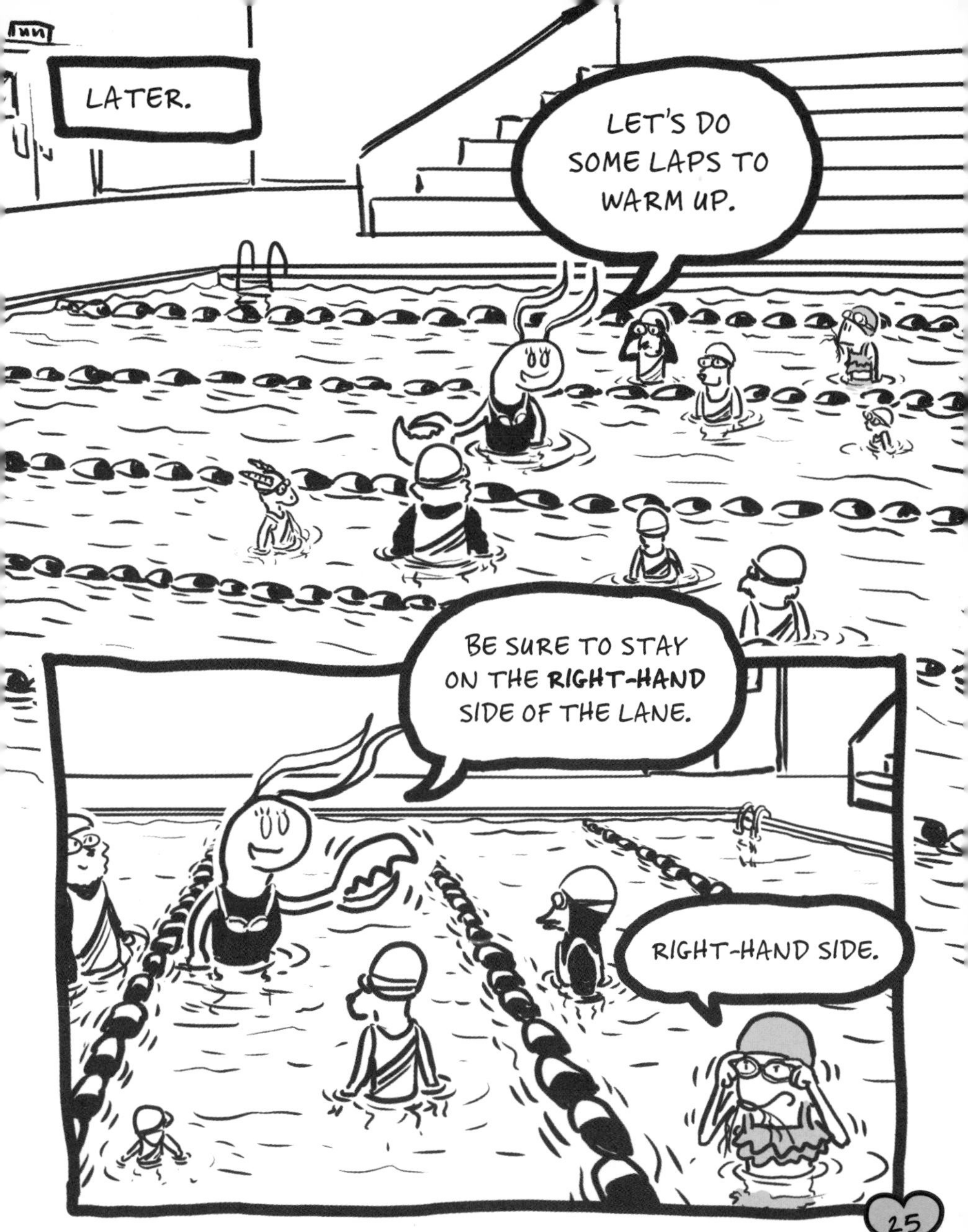
LATER.
LET'S DO SOME LAPS TO WARM UP.
BE SURE TO STAY ON THE **RIGHT-HAND** SIDE OF THE LANE.
RIGHT-HAND SIDE.

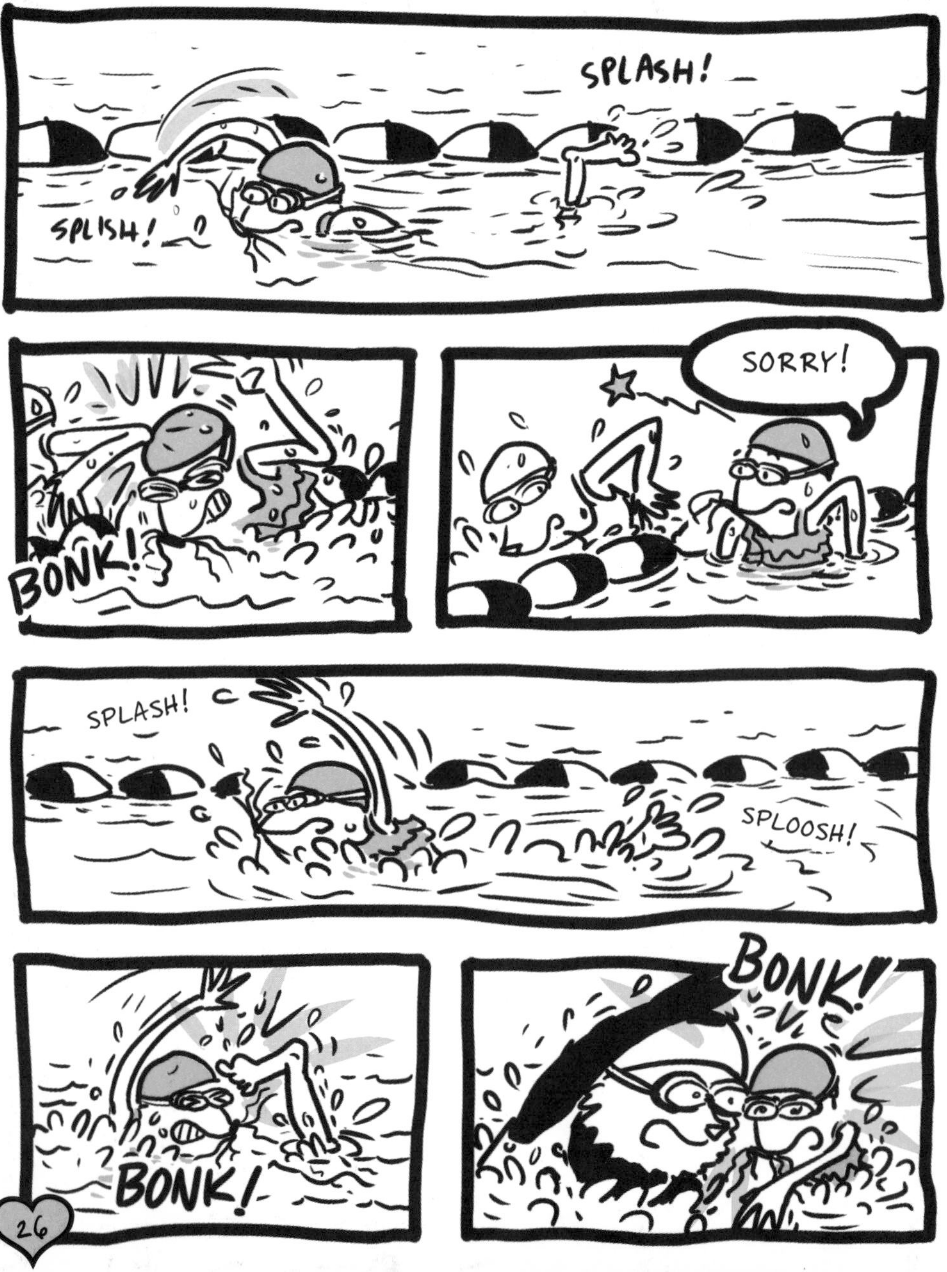
SPLASH!
SPLISH!
BONK!
SORRY!
SPLASH!
SPLOOSH!
BONK!
BONK!

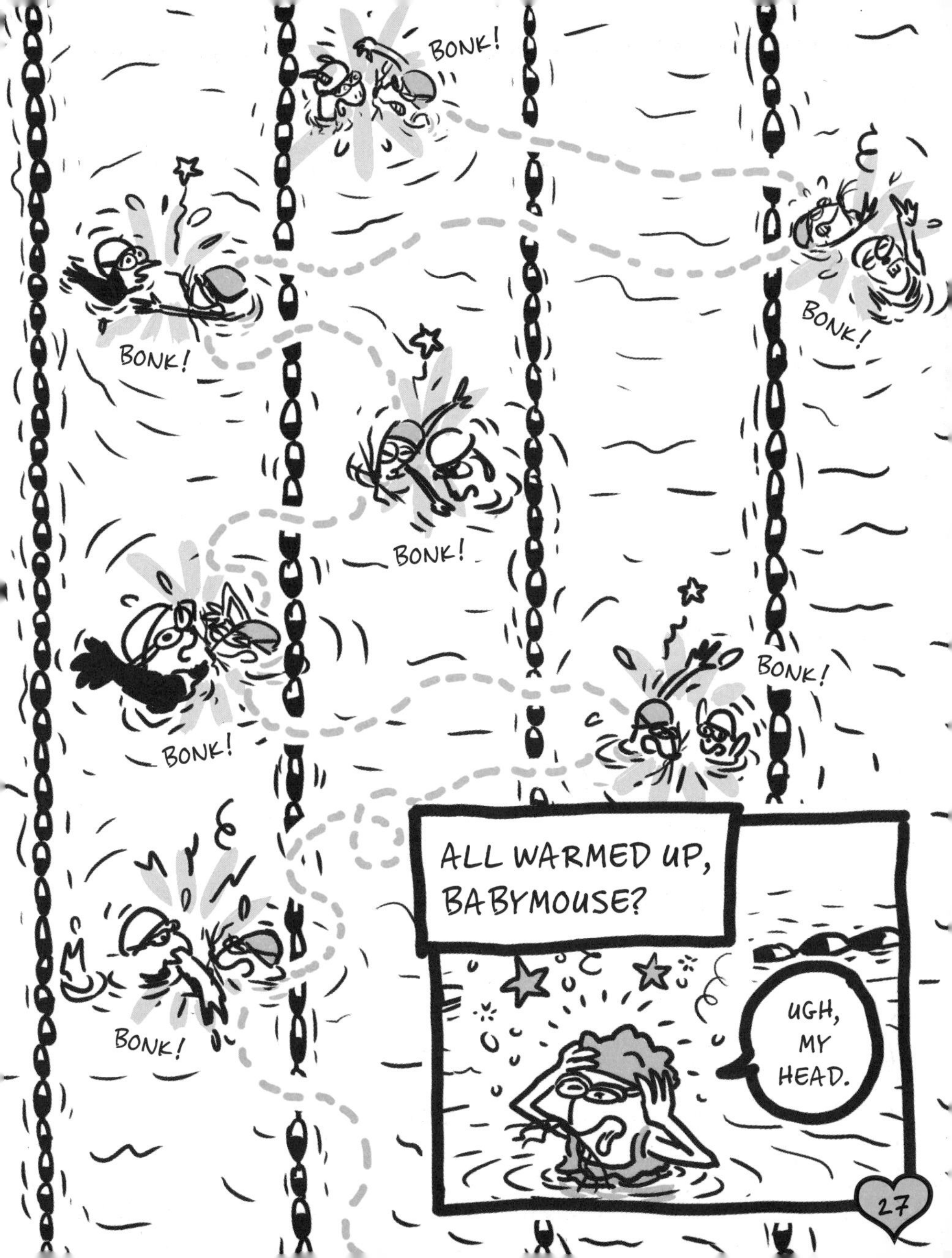
BONK!
BONK!
BONK!
BONK!
BONK!
BONK!
BONK!
ALL WARMED UP, BABYMOUSE?
UGH, MY HEAD.

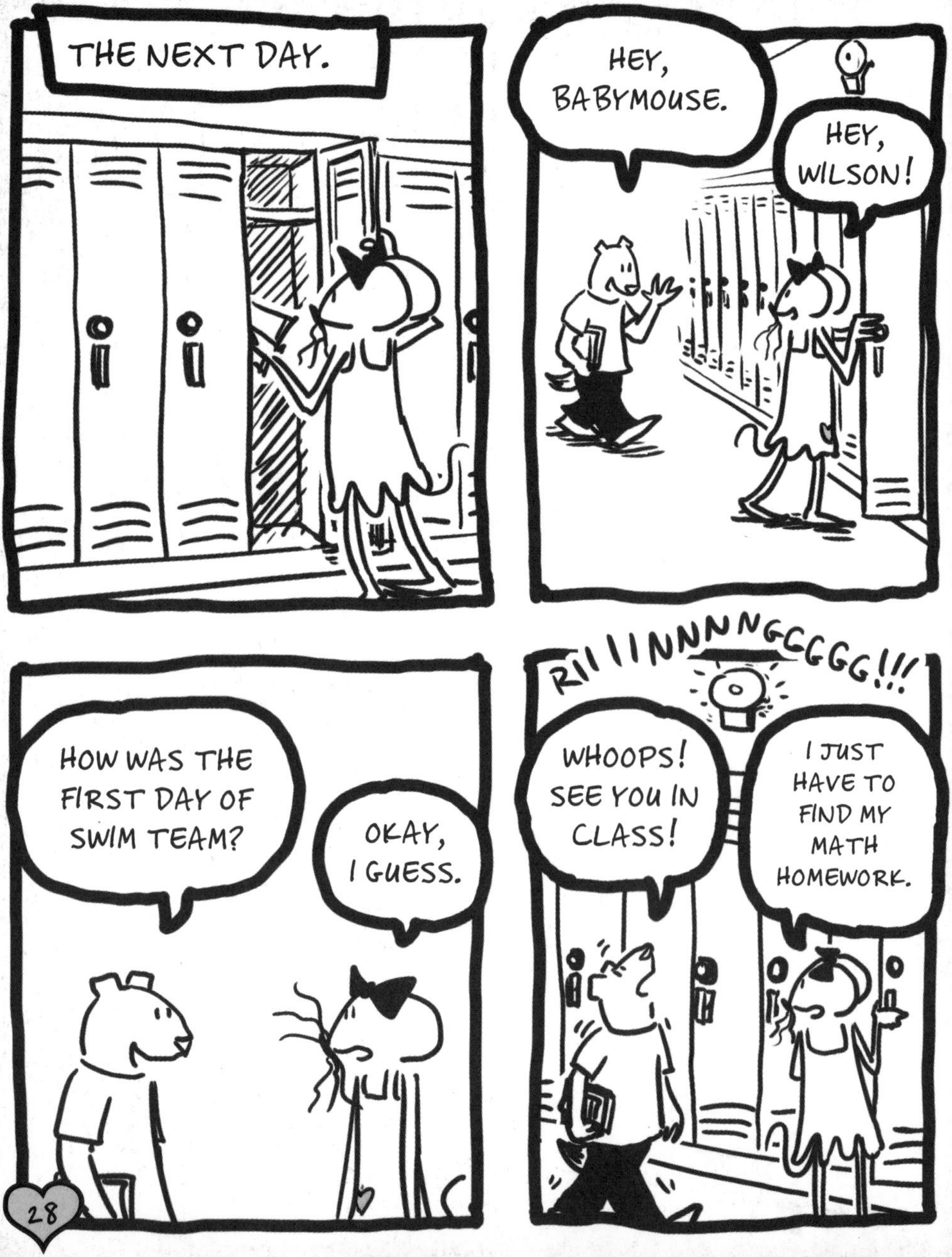

THE NEXT DAY.
HEY, BABYMOUSE.
HEY, WILSON!
HOW WAS THE FIRST DAY OF SWIM TEAM?
OKAY, I GUESS.
RIIIINNNNGGGGG!!!
WHOOPS! SEE YOU IN CLASS!
I JUST HAVE TO FIND MY MATH HOMEWORK.

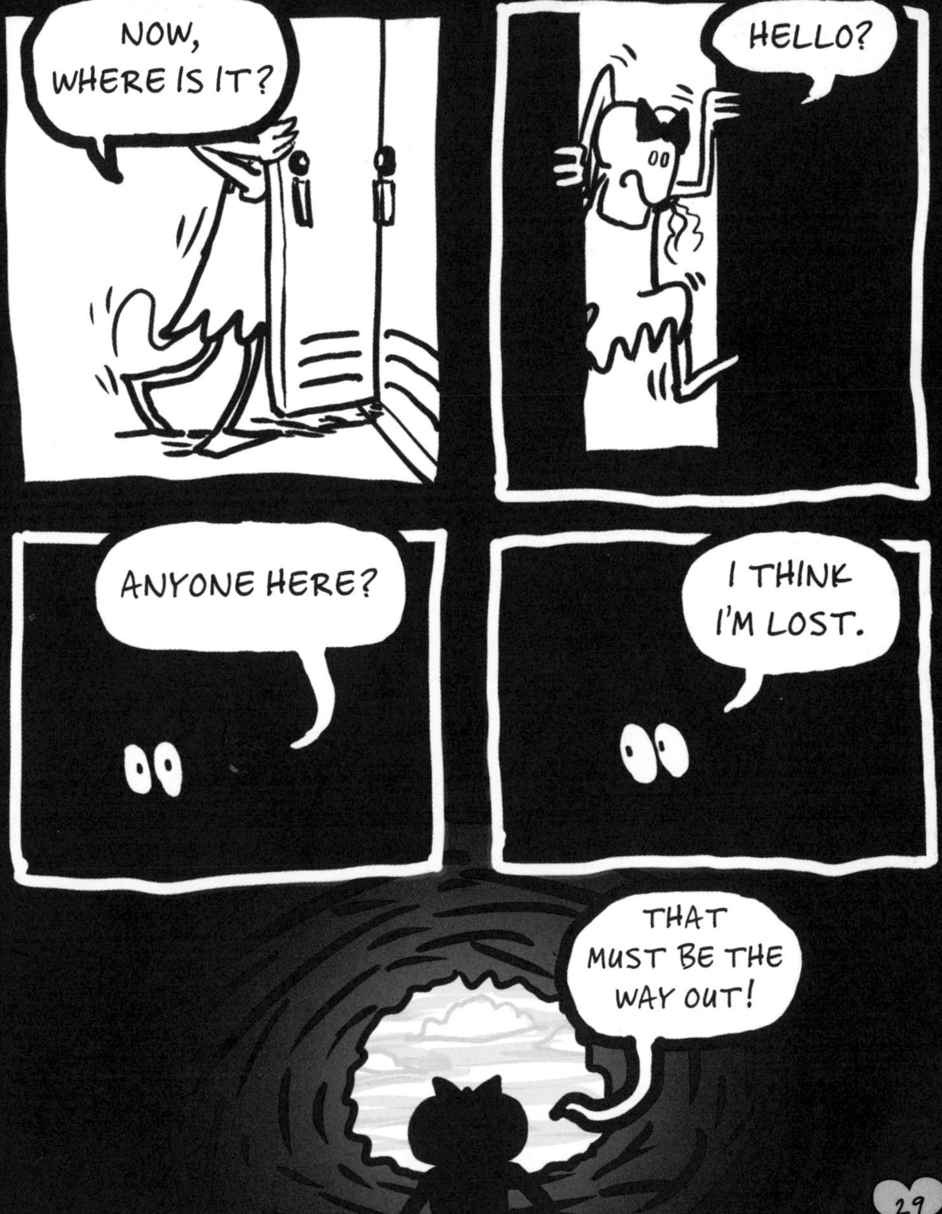
NOW, WHERE IS IT?
HELLO?
ANYONE HERE?
I THINK I'M LOST.
THAT MUST BE THE WAY OUT!

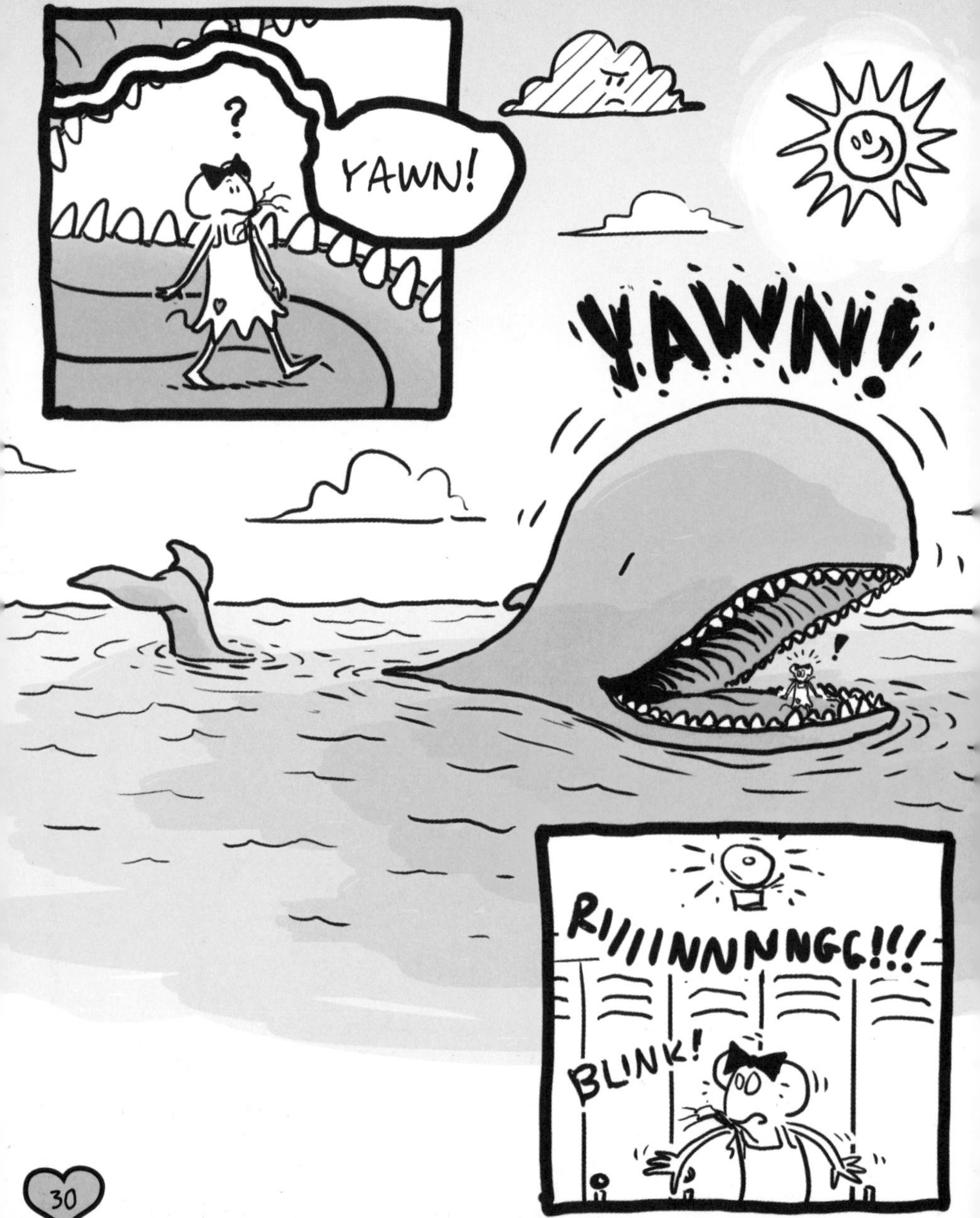
?
YAWN!
YAWN!
!
RIIIINNNNGG!!!
BLINK!

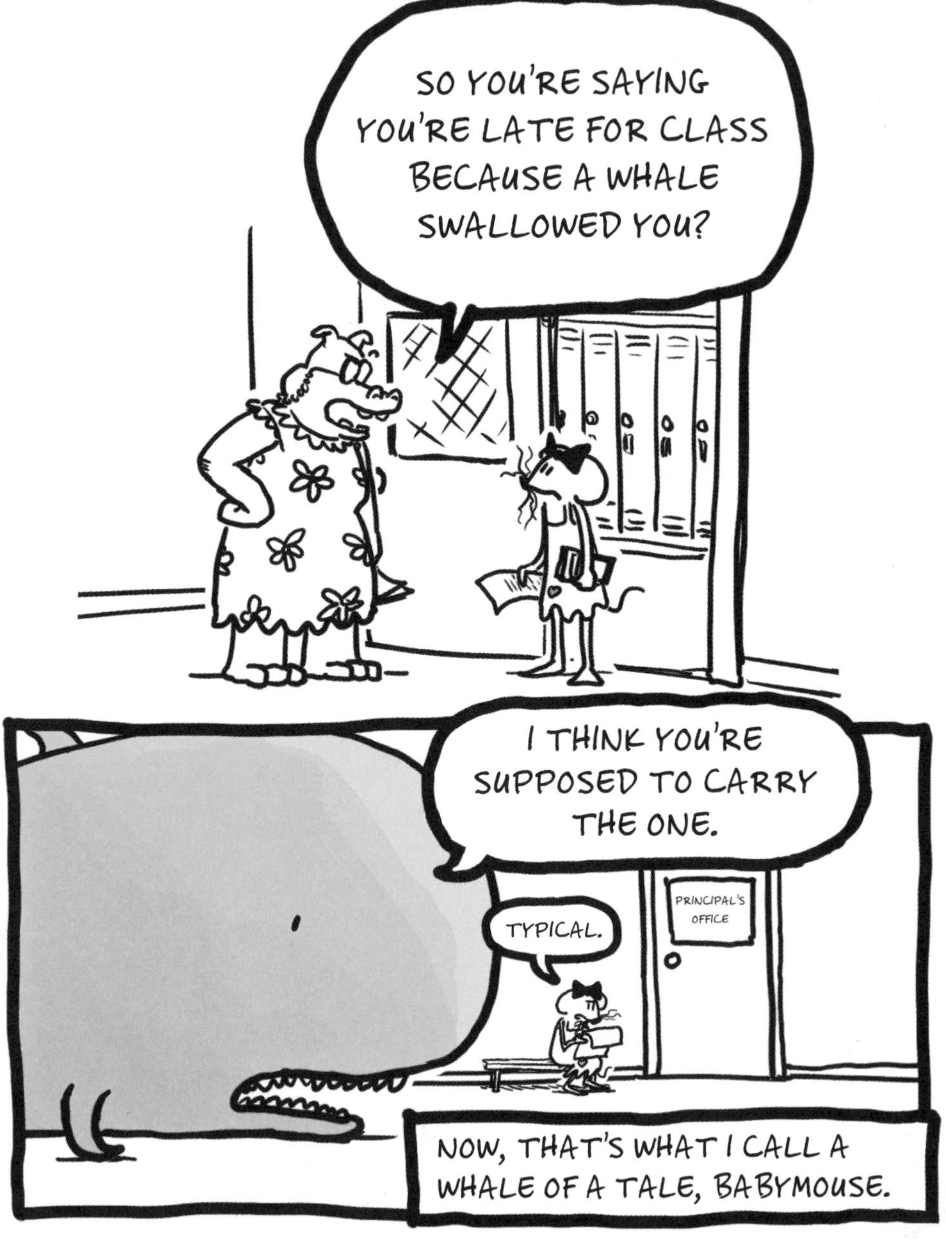
SO YOU'RE SAYING YOU'RE LATE FOR CLASS BECAUSE A WHALE SWALLOWED YOU?
I THINK YOU'RE SUPPOSED TO CARRY THE ONE.
PRINCIPAL'S OFFICE
TYPICAL.
NOW, THAT'S WHAT I CALL A WHALE OF A TALE, BABYMOUSE.

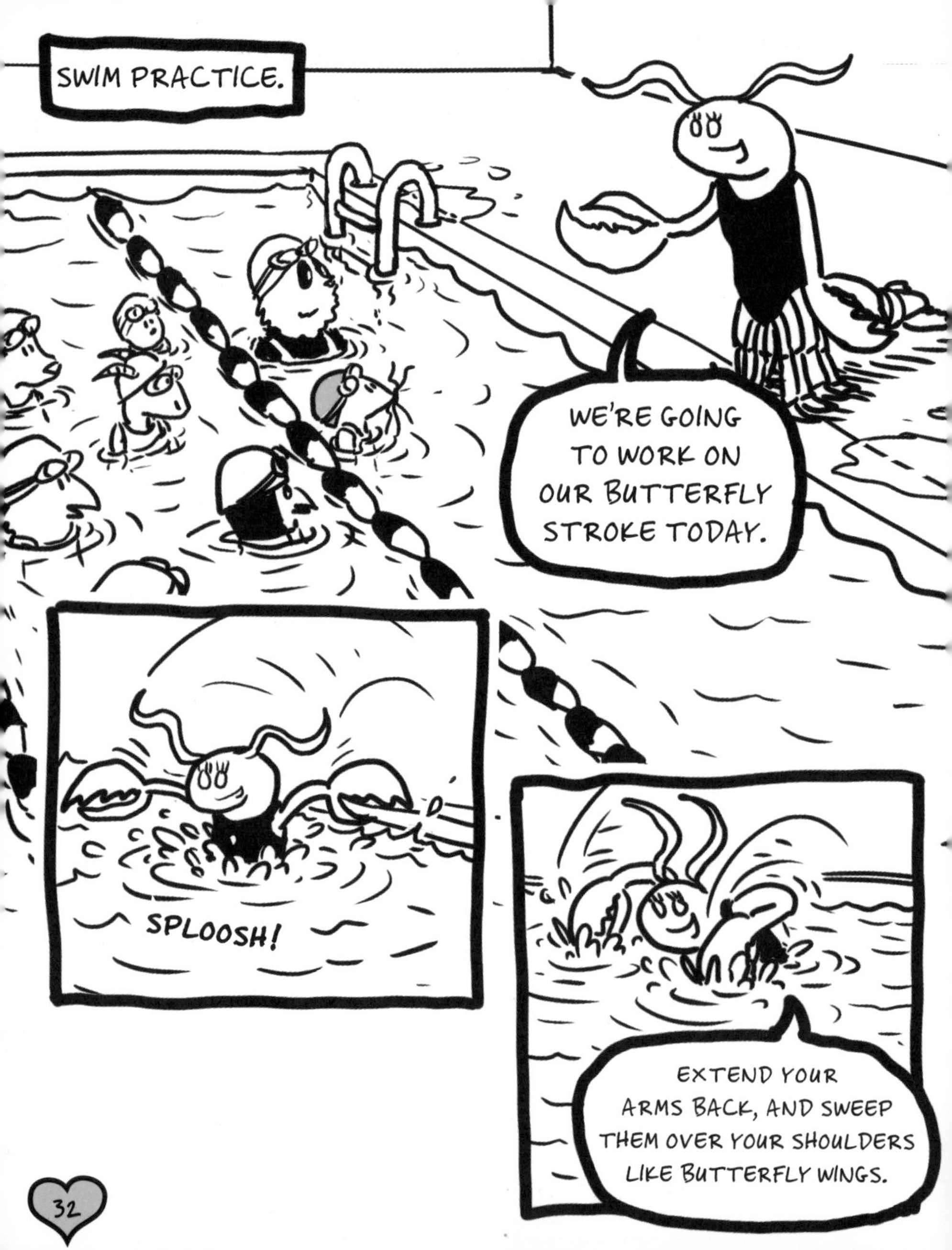
SWIM PRACTICE.
WE'RE GOING TO WORK ON OUR BUTTERFLY STROKE TODAY.
SPLOOSH!
EXTEND YOUR ARMS BACK, AND SWEEP THEM OVER YOUR SHOULDERS LIKE BUTTERFLY WINGS.

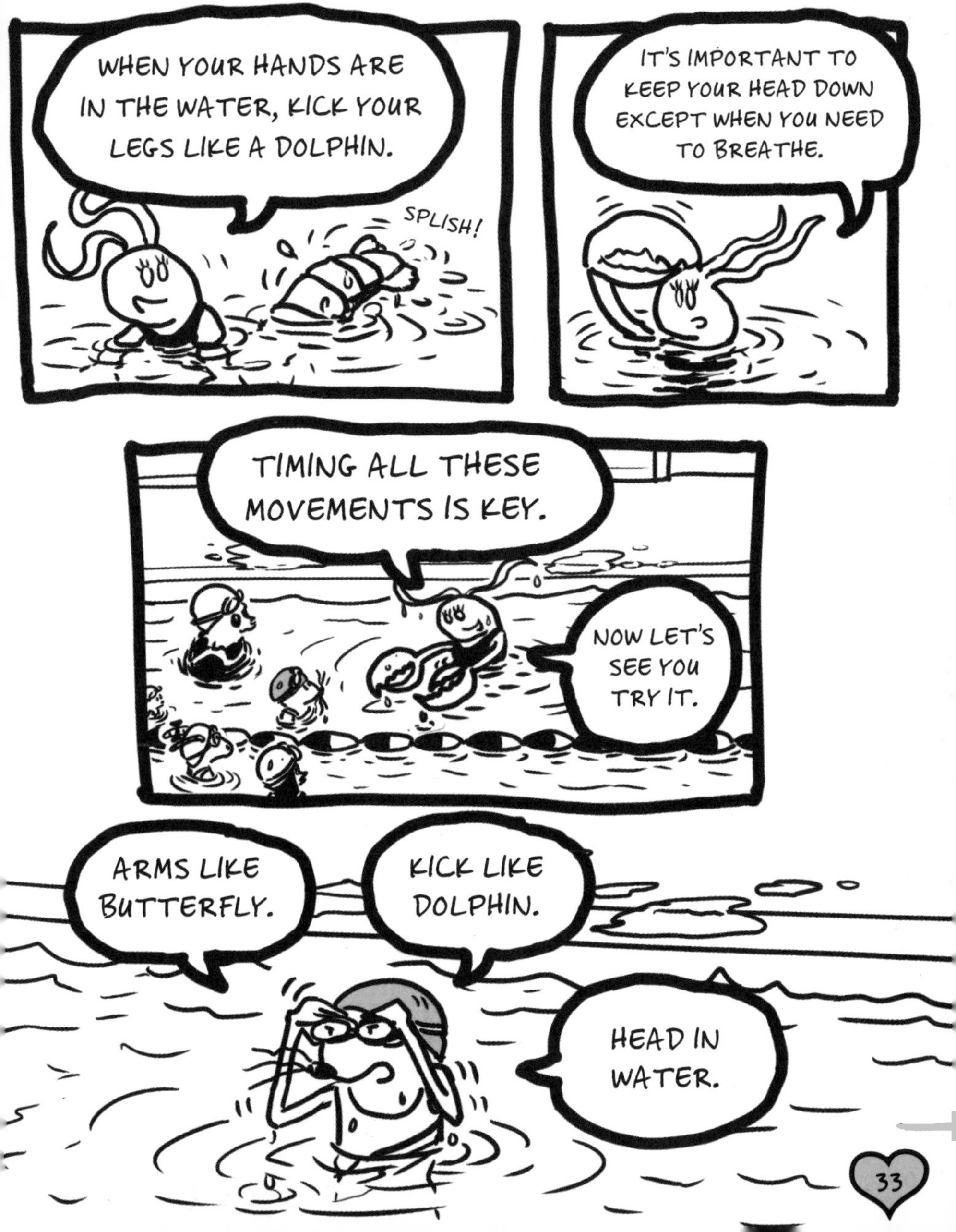

WHEN YOUR HANDS ARE IN THE WATER, KICK YOUR LEGS LIKE A DOLPHIN.
SPLISH!
IT'S IMPORTANT TO KEEP YOUR HEAD DOWN EXCEPT WHEN YOU NEED TO BREATHE.
TIMING ALL THESE MOVEMENTS IS KEY.
NOW LET'S SEE YOU TRY IT.
ARMS LIKE BUTTERFLY.
KICK LIKE DOLPHIN.
HEAD IN WATER.

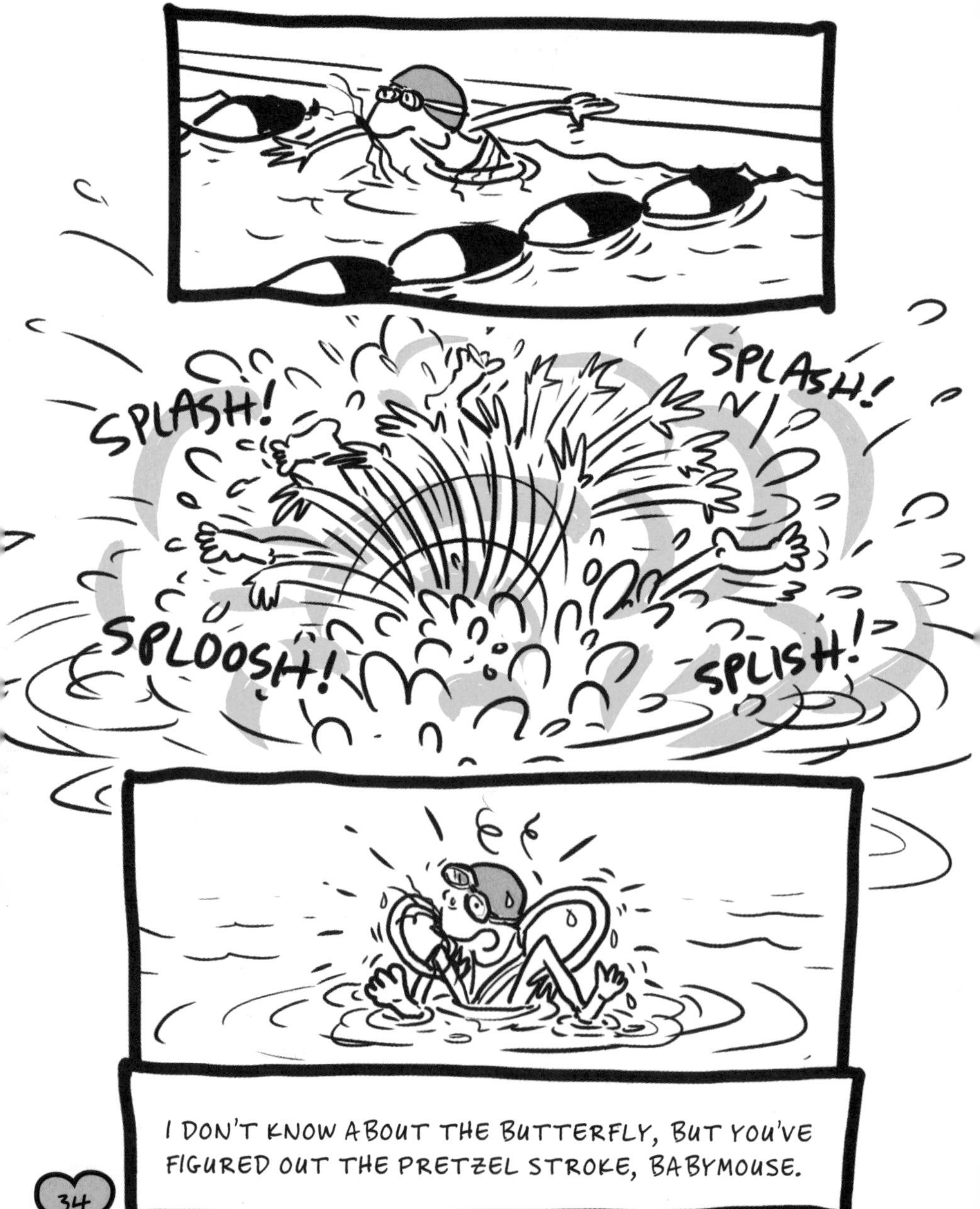
SPLASH!
SPLASH!
SPLOOSH!
SPLISH!
I DON'T KNOW ABOUT THE BUTTERFLY, BUT YOU'VE FIGURED OUT THE PRETZEL STROKE, BABYMOUSE.

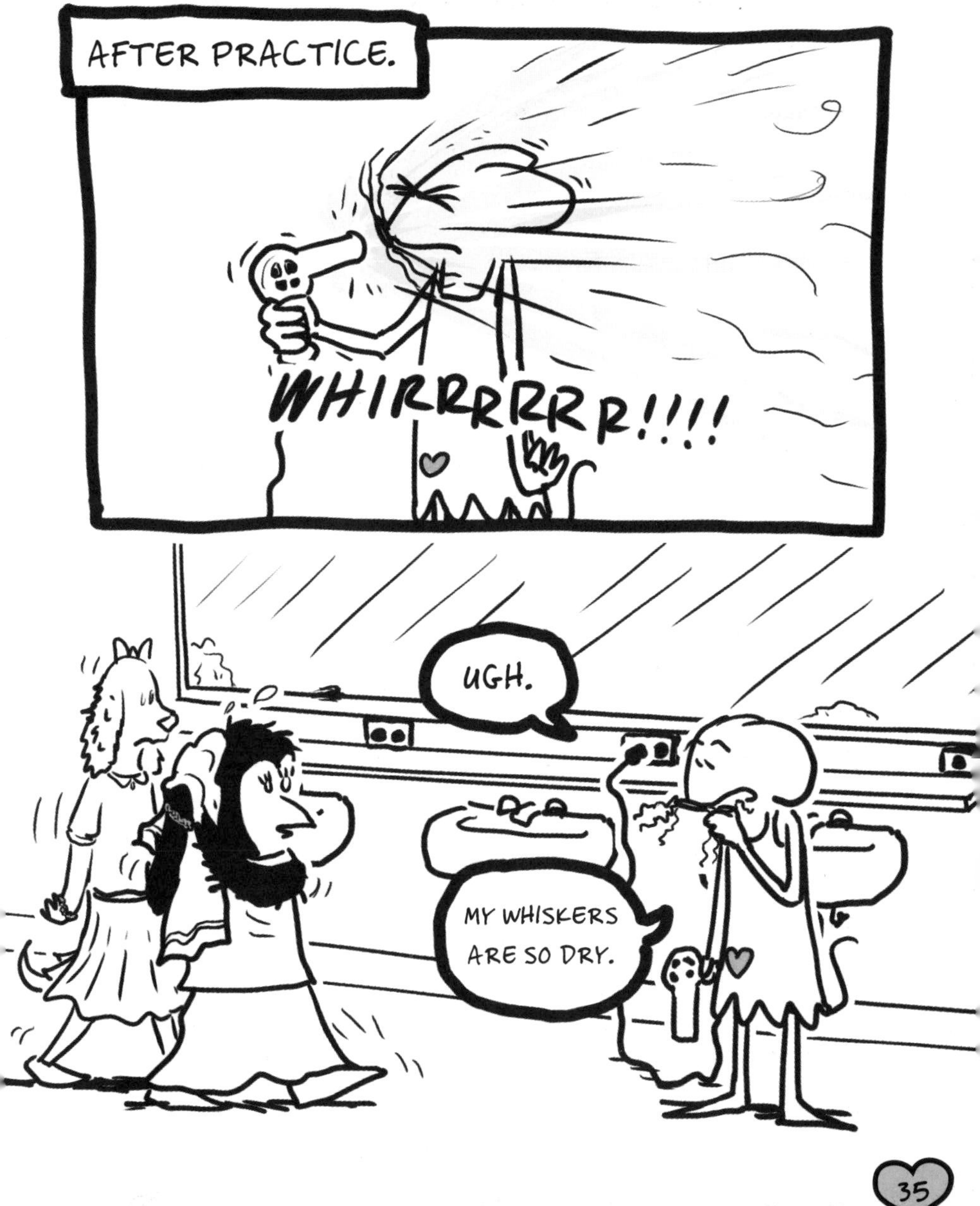
AFTER PRACTICE.
WHIRRRRRRR!!!!
UGH.
MY WHISKERS ARE SO DRY.

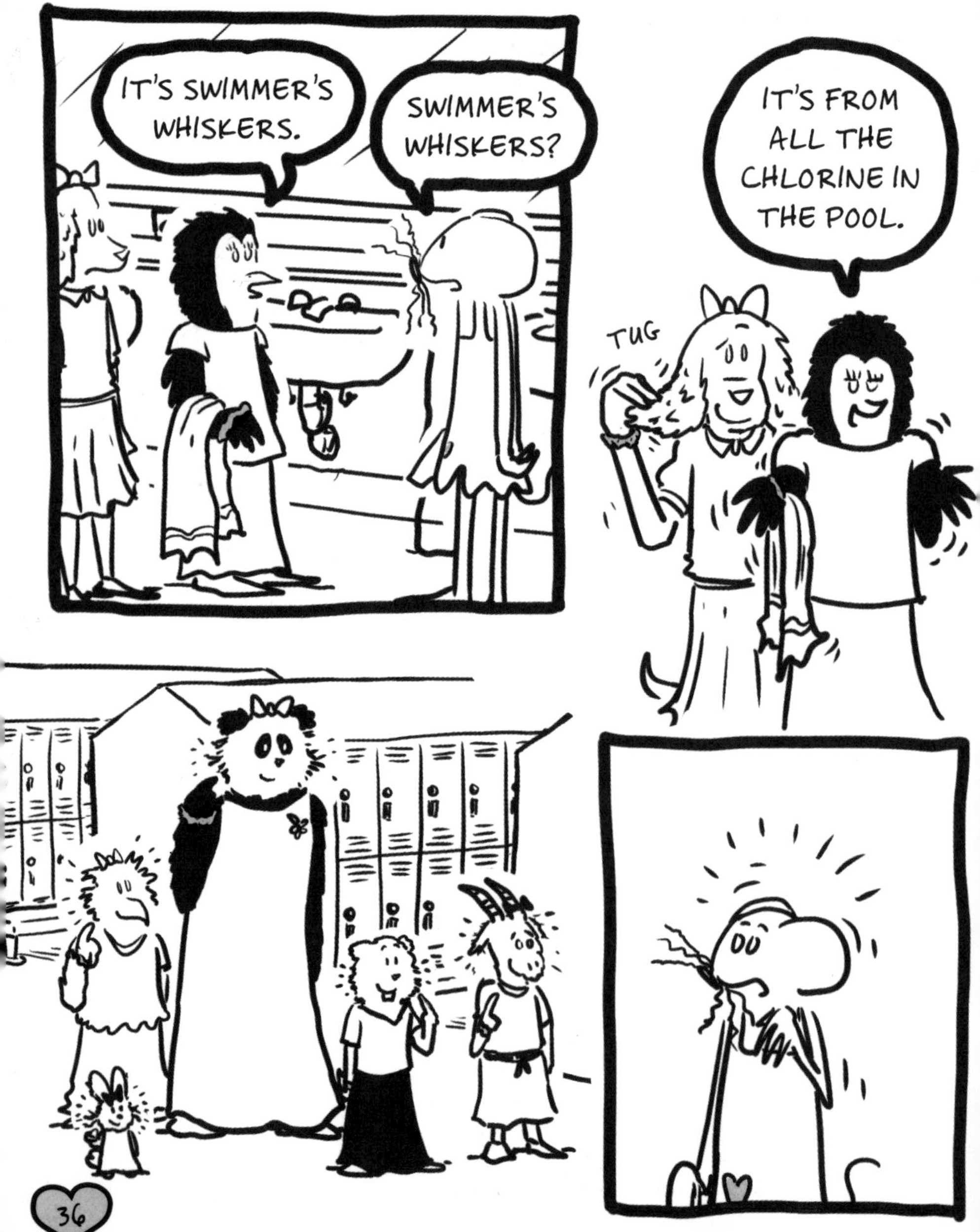
IT'S SWIMMER'S WHISKERS.
SWIMMER'S WHISKERS?
IT'S FROM ALL THE CHLORINE IN THE POOL.
TUG

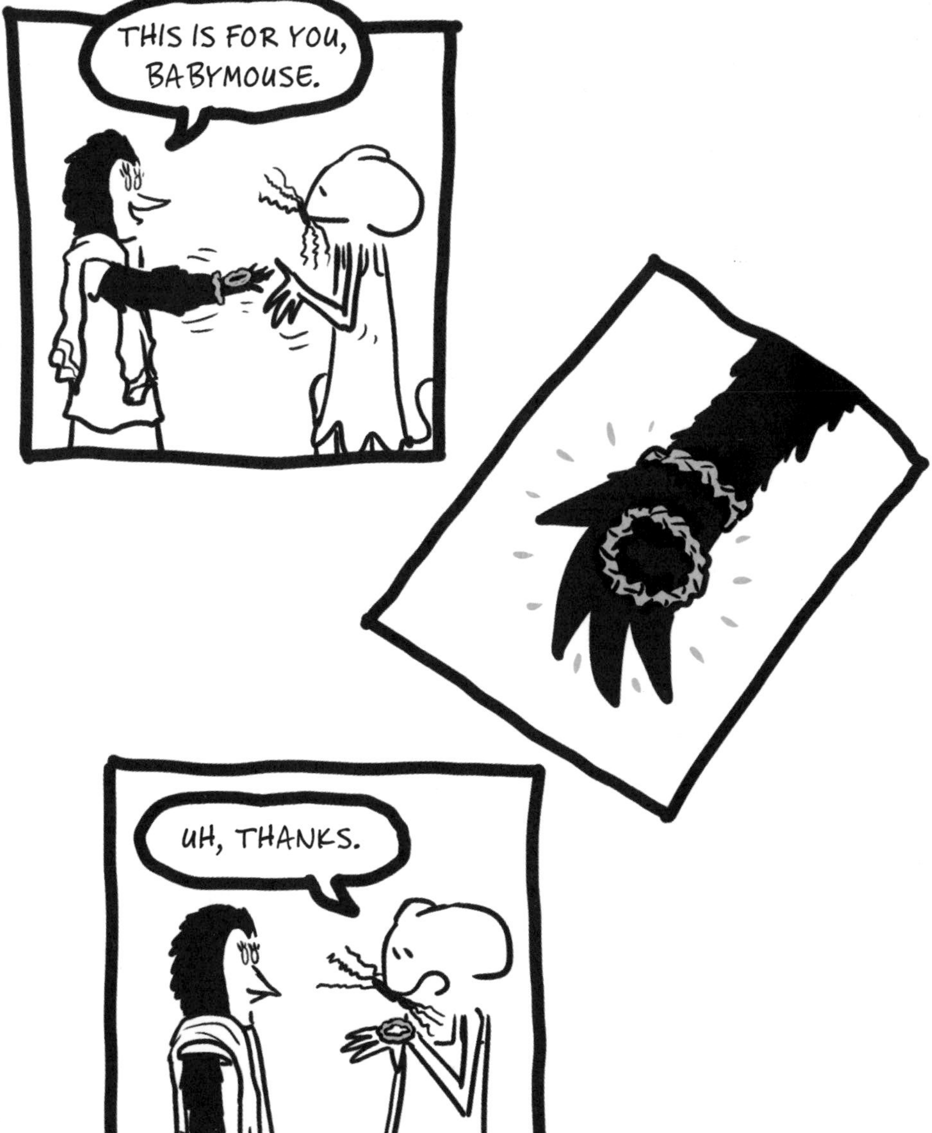
THIS IS FOR YOU, BABYMOUSE.
UH, THANKS.

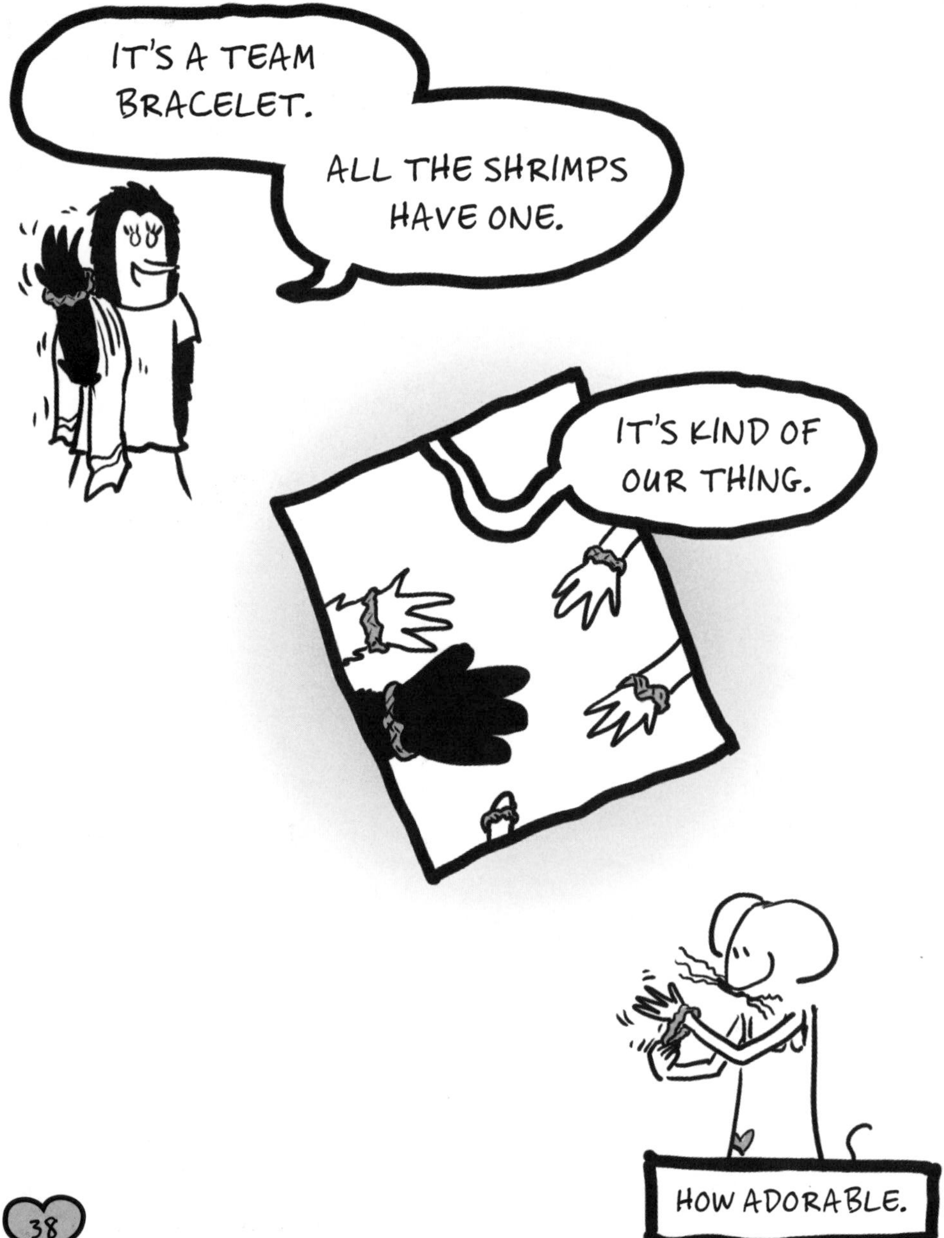
IT'S A TEAM BRACELET.
ALL THE SHRIMPS HAVE ONE.
IT'S KIND OF OUR THING.
HOW ADORABLE.

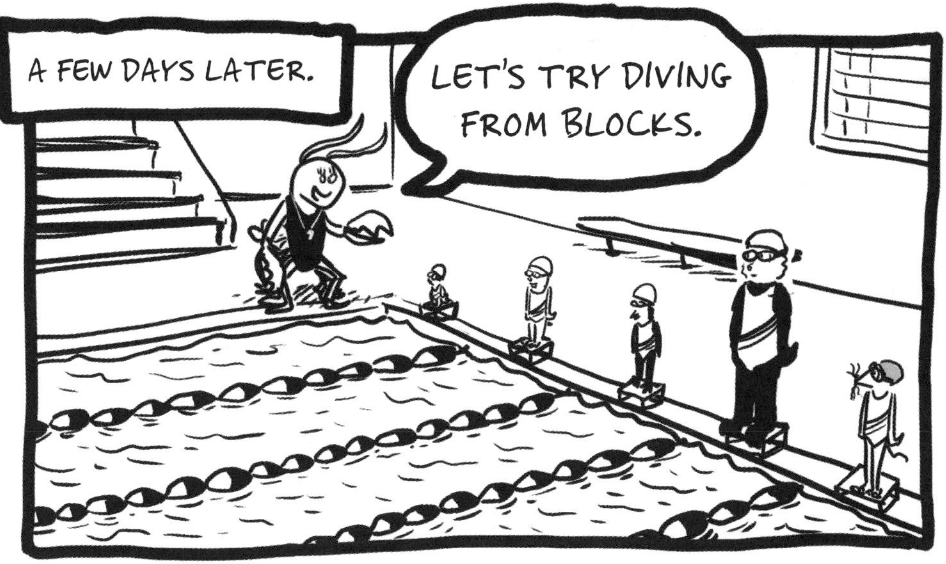
A FEW DAYS LATER.
LET'S TRY DIVING FROM BLOCKS.

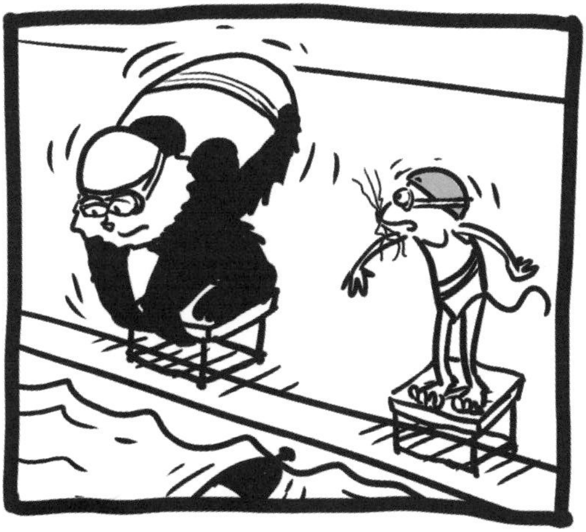

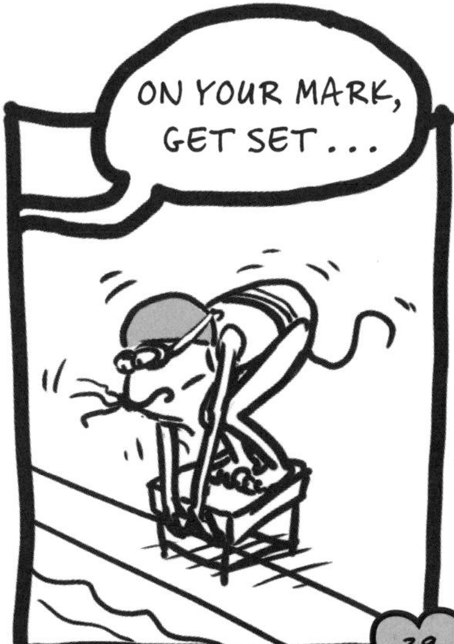
ON YOUR MARK, GET SET . . .

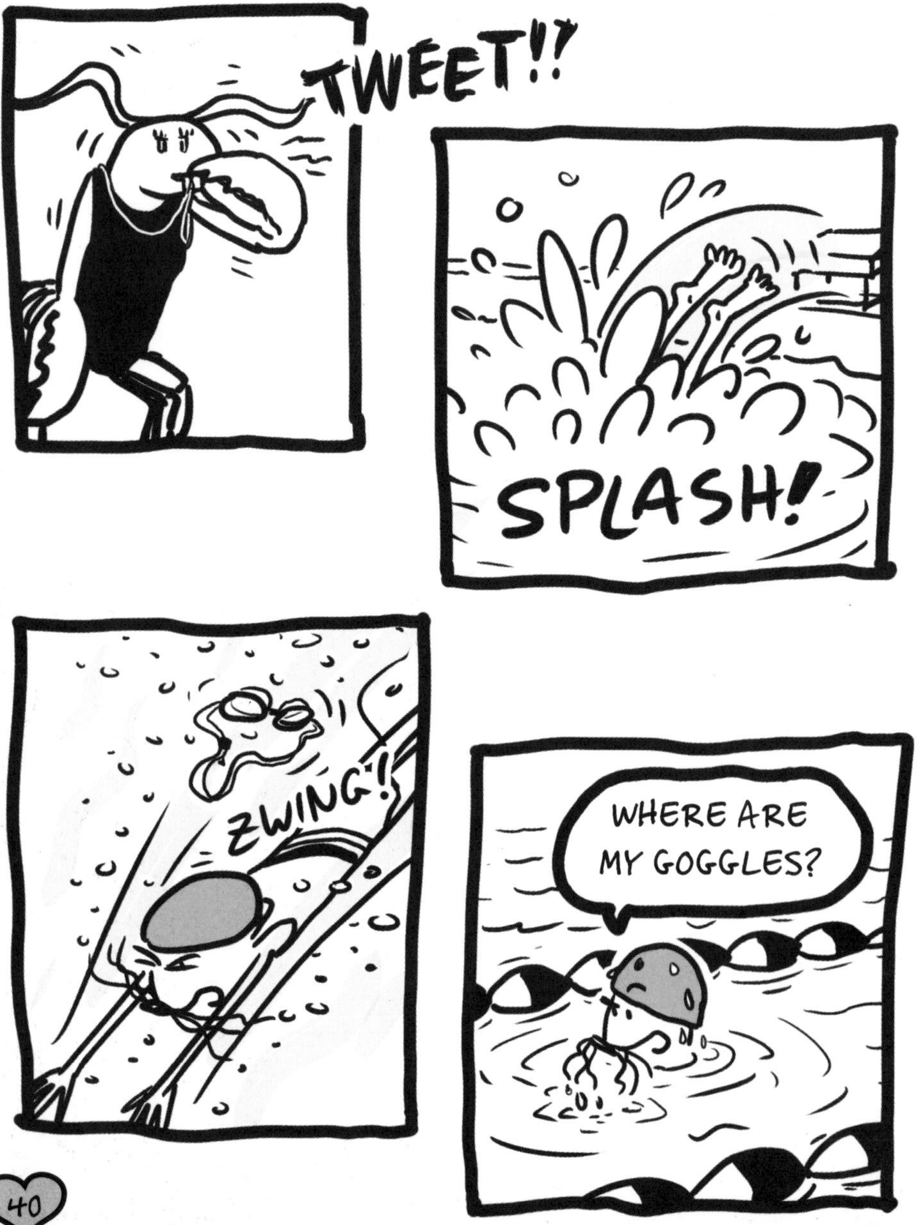
TWEET!!
SPLASH!
ZWING!
WHERE ARE MY GOGGLES?

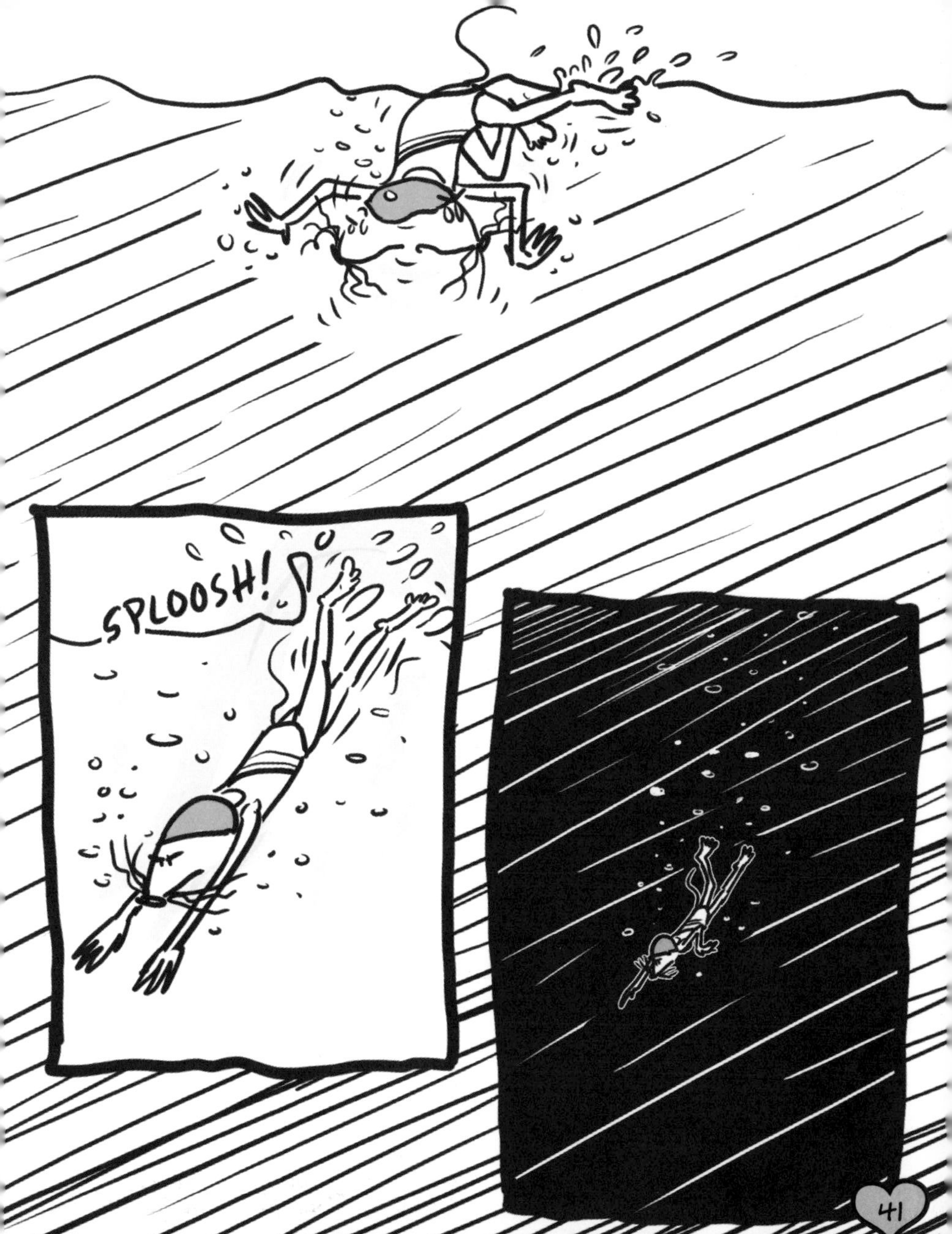
SPLOOSH!

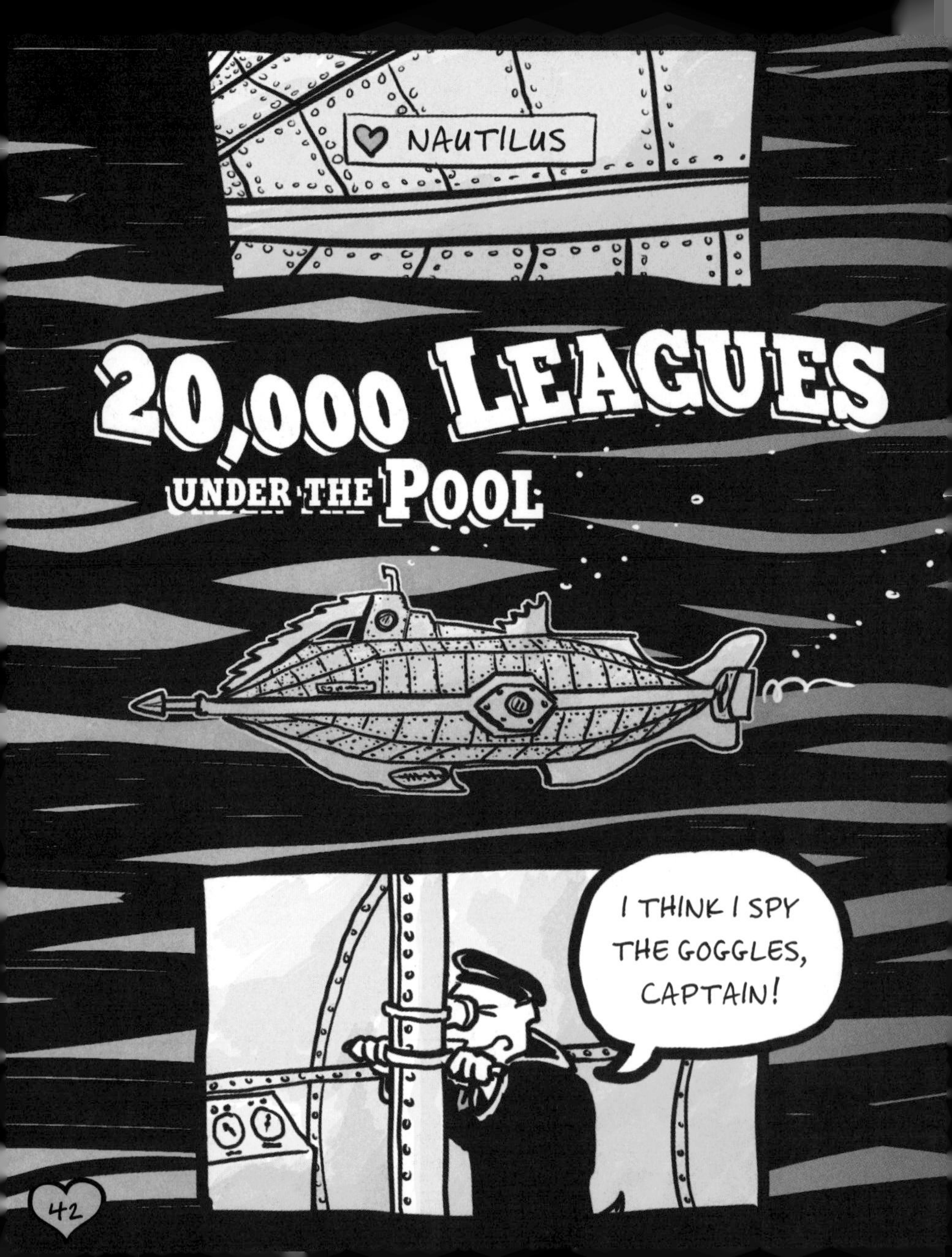
NAUTILUS
20,000 LEAGUES UNDER THE POOL
I THINK I SPY THE GOGGLES, CAPTAIN!

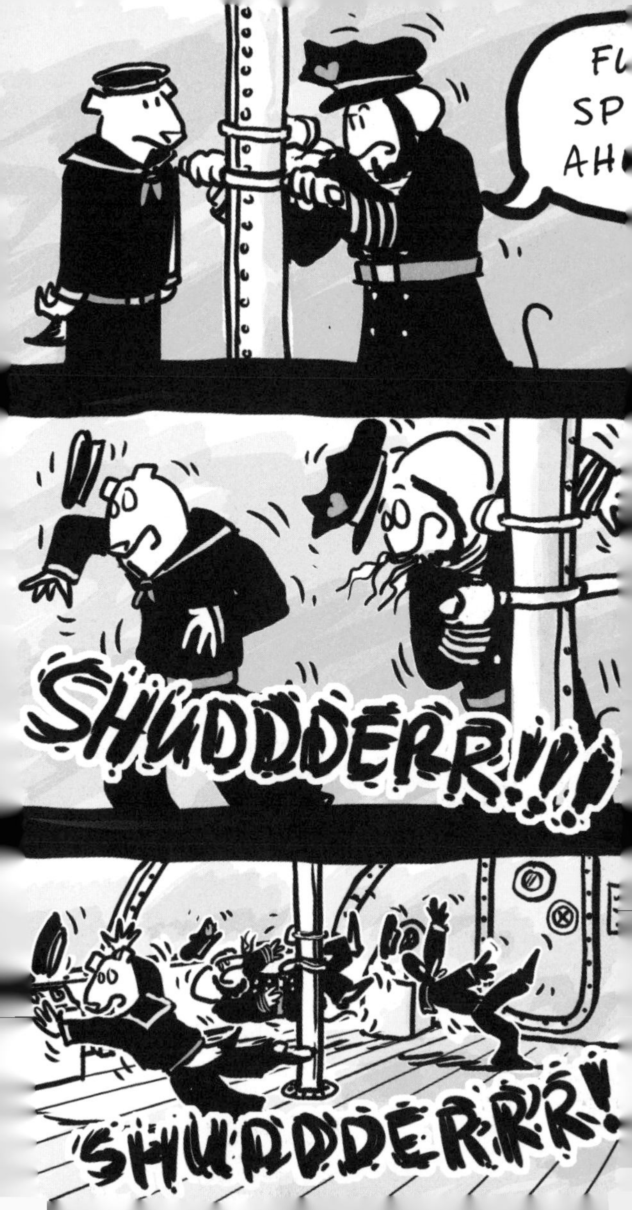
SHUDDDERR!!!
SHUDDDERRRR!

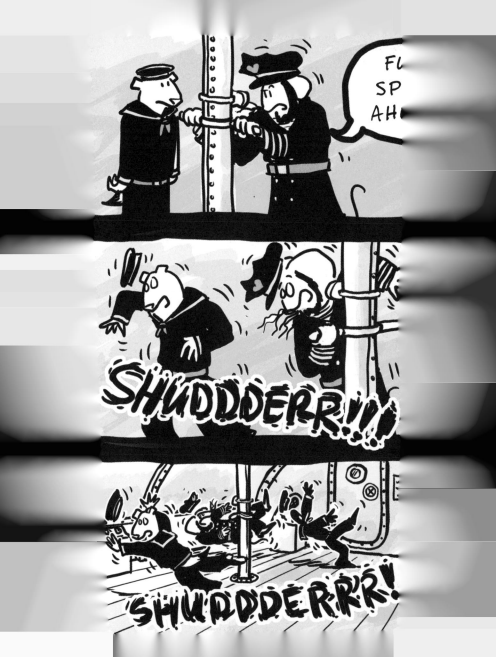

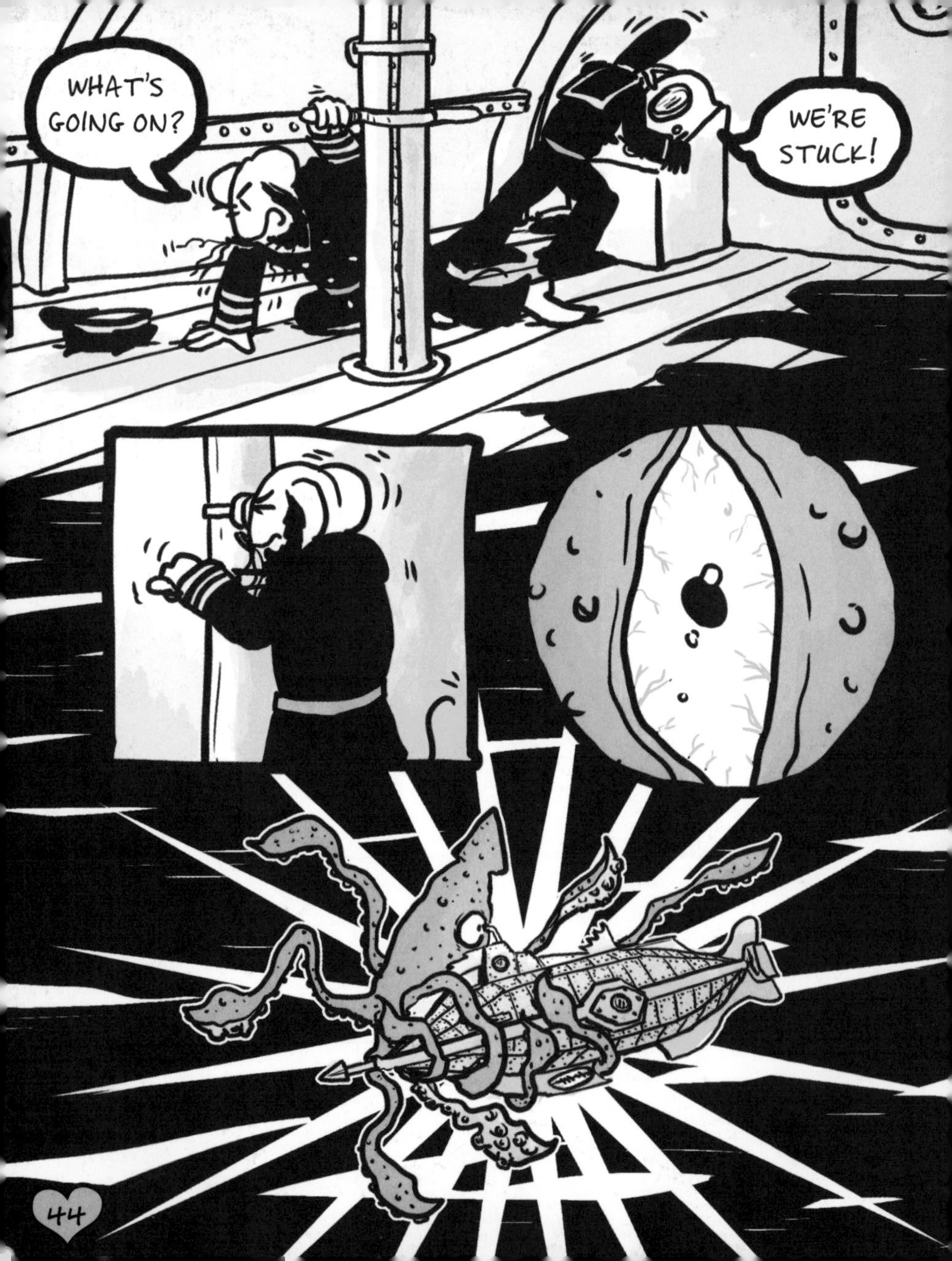

WHAT'S GOING ON?
WE'RE STUCK!

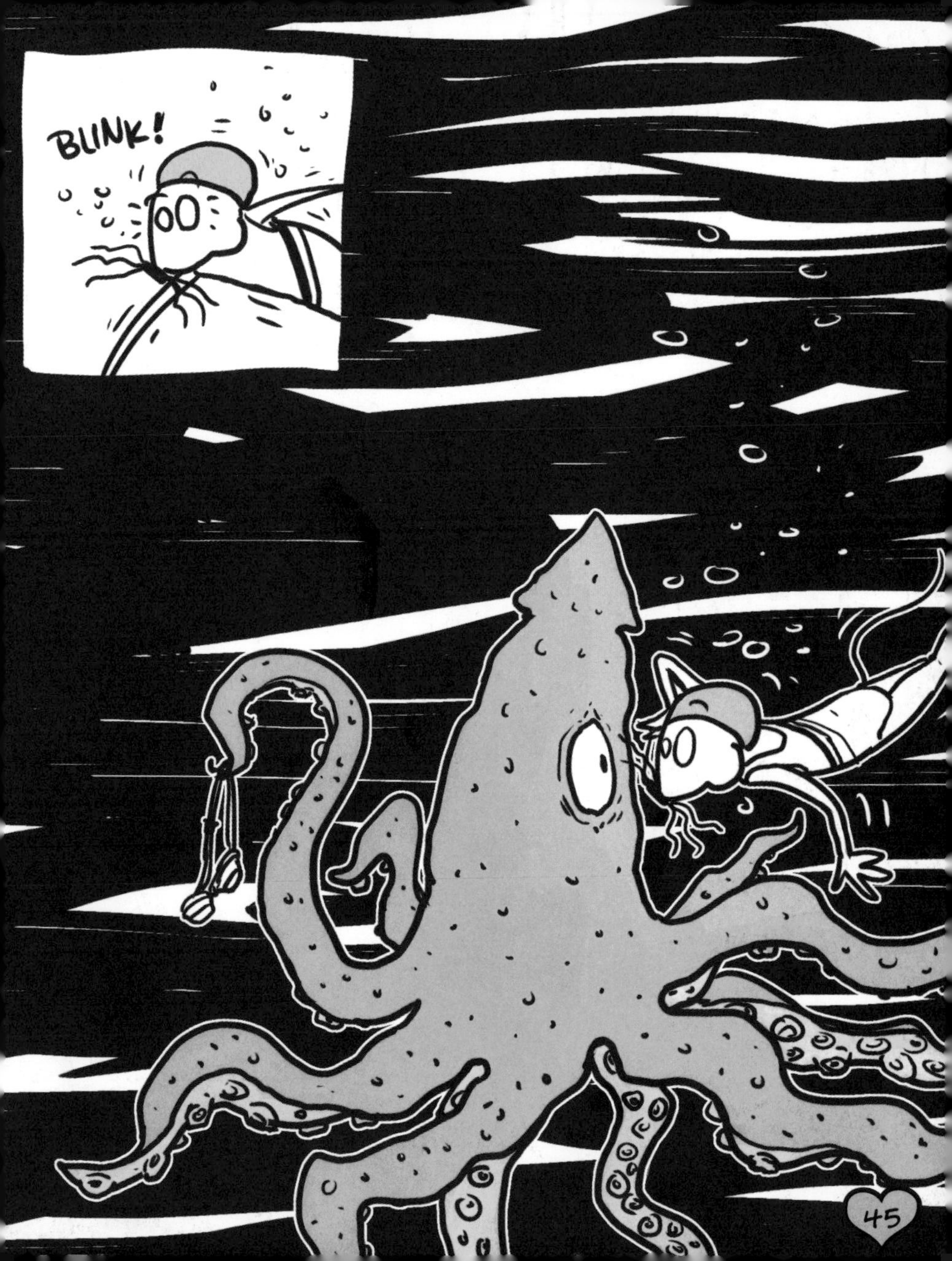
BLINK!

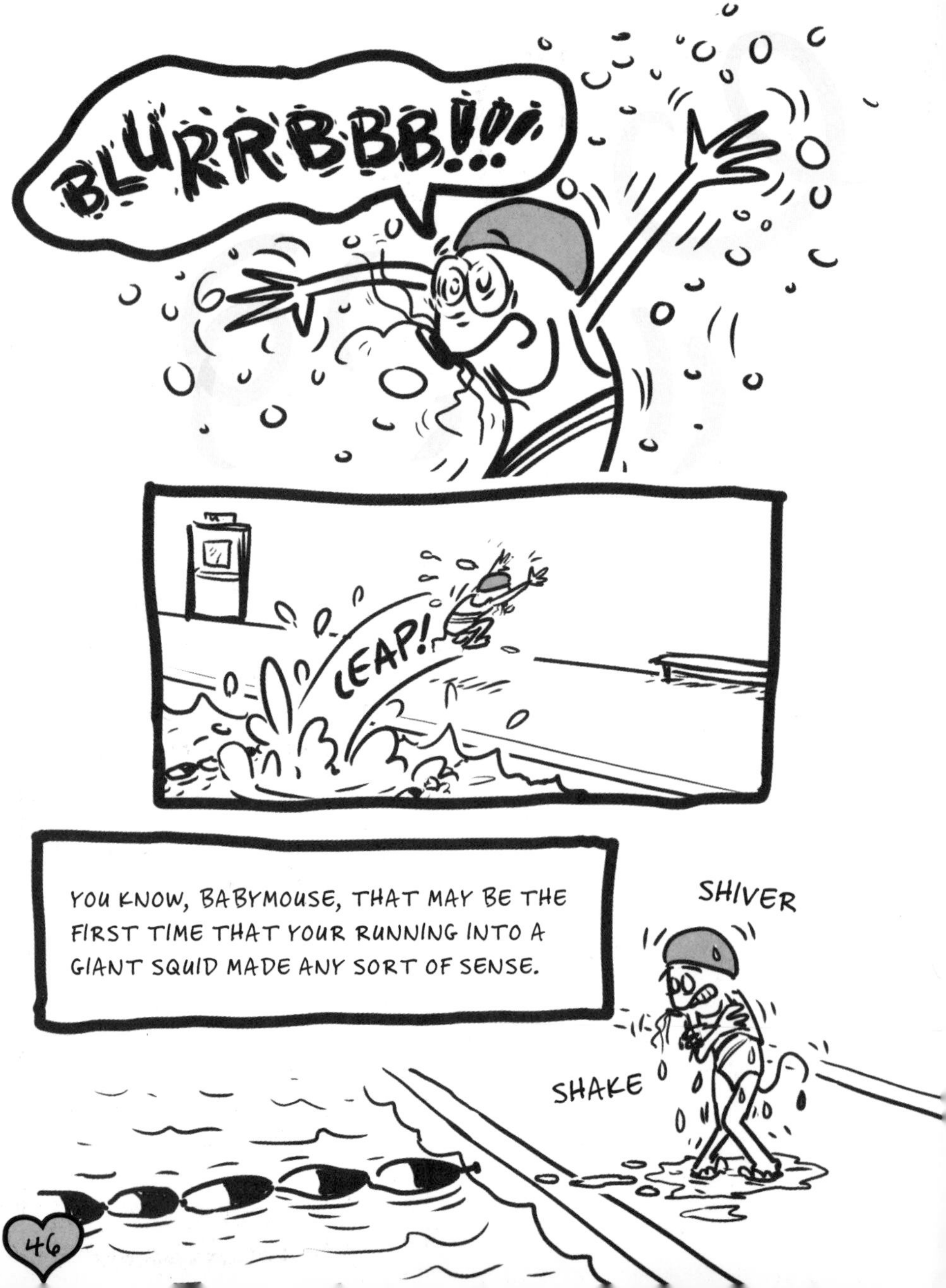
BLURRBBB!!!
LEAP!
YOU KNOW, BABYMOUSE, THAT MAY BE THE FIRST TIME THAT YOUR RUNNING INTO A GIANT SQUID MADE ANY SORT OF SENSE.
SHIVER
SHAKE

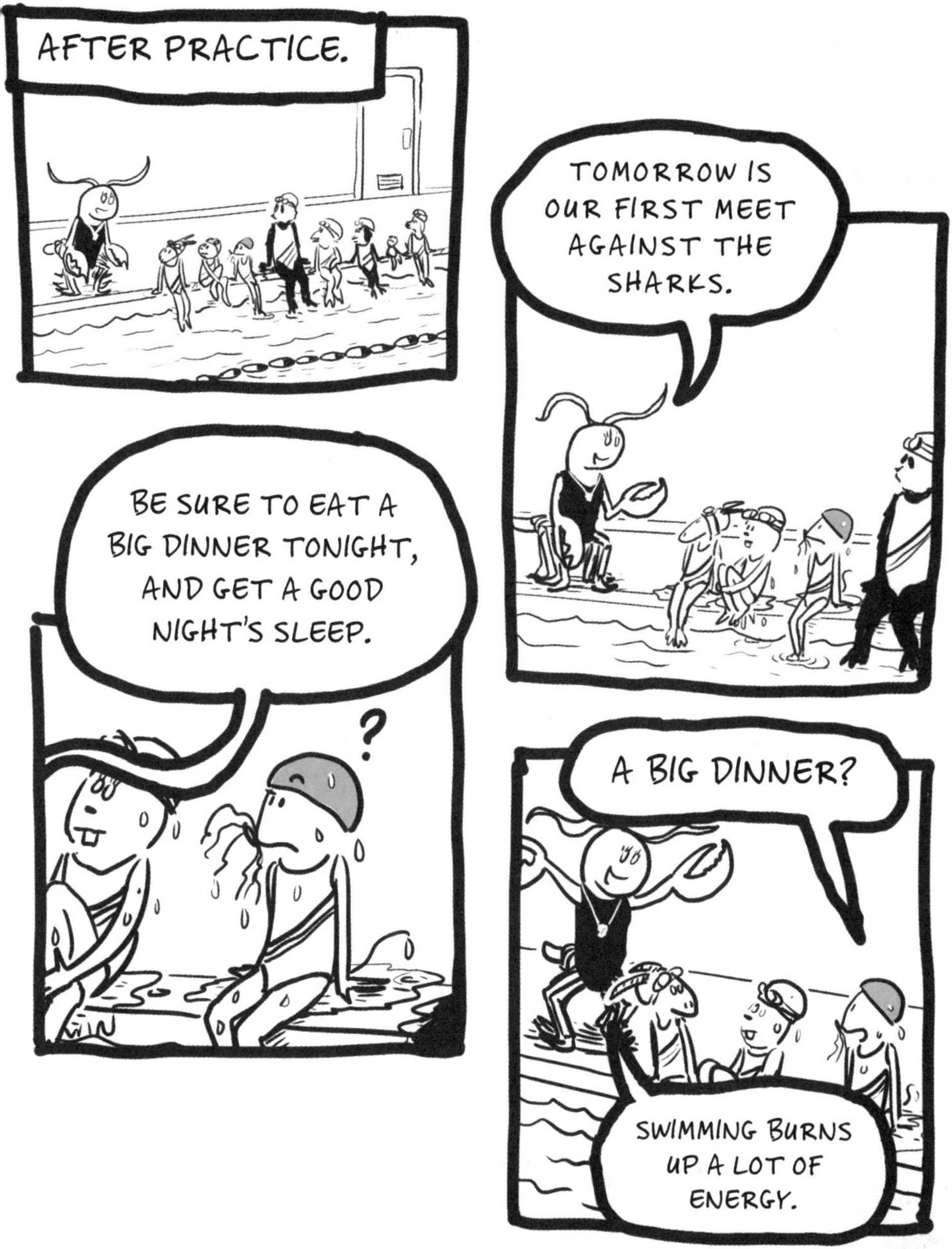
AFTER PRACTICE.
TOMORROW IS OUR FIRST MEET AGAINST THE SHARKS.
BE SURE TO EAT A BIG DINNER TONIGHT, AND GET A GOOD NIGHT'S SLEEP.
?
A BIG DINNER?
SWIMMING BURNS UP A LOT OF ENERGY.

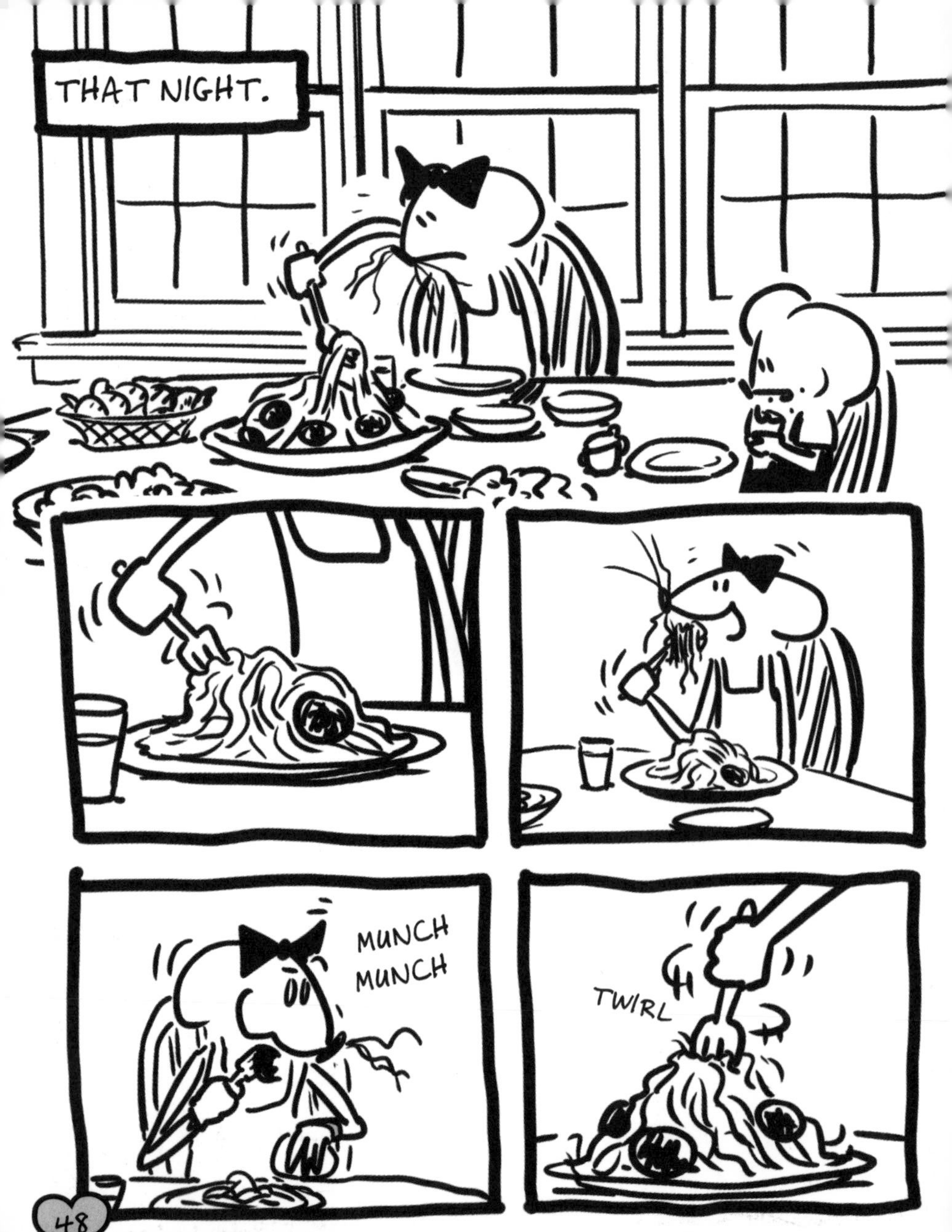
THAT NIGHT.
MUNCH
MUNCH
TWIRL

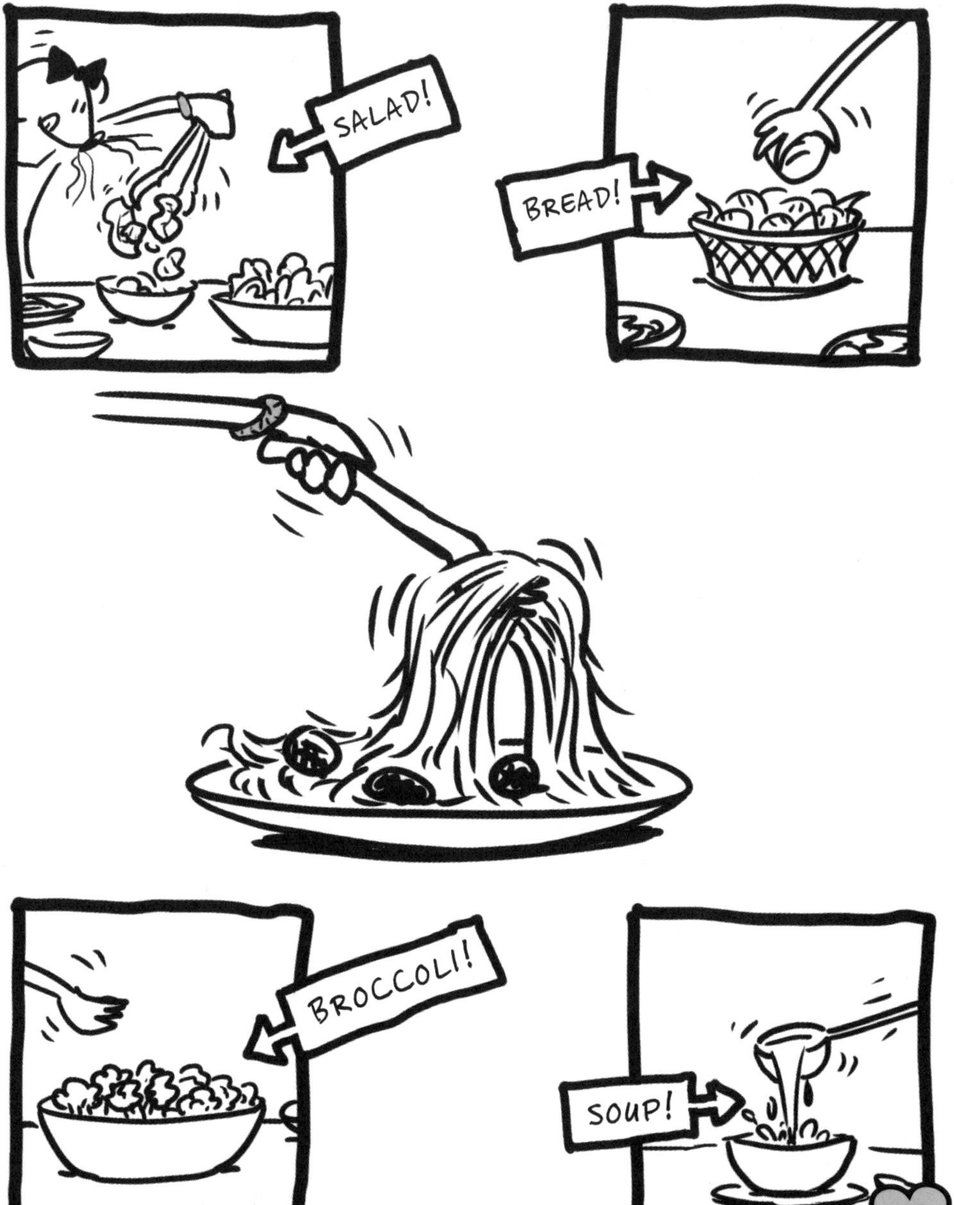
SALAD!
BREAD!
BROCCOLI!
SOUP!

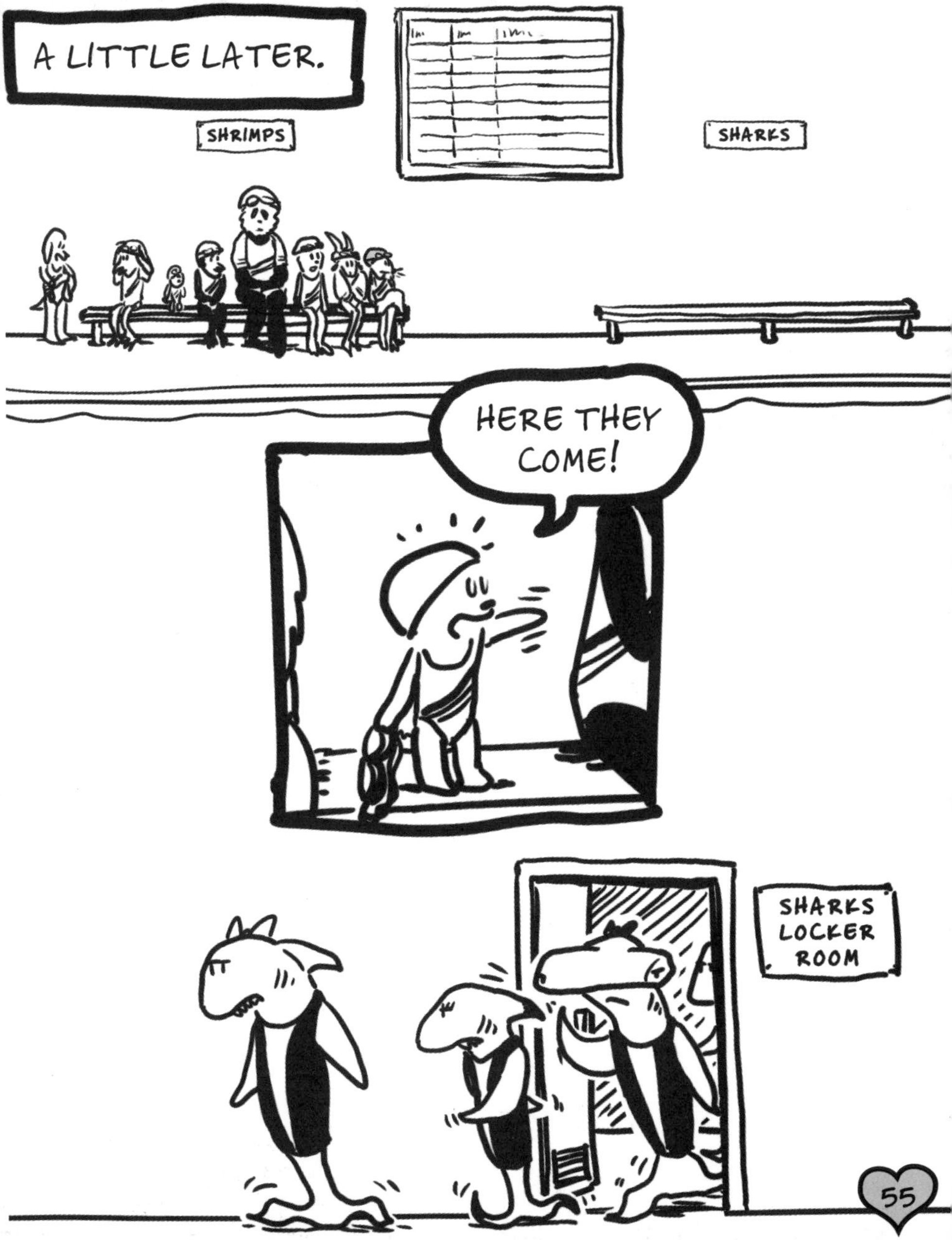
A LITTLE LATER.
SHRIMPS
SHARKS
HERE THEY COME!
SHARKS LOCKER ROOM

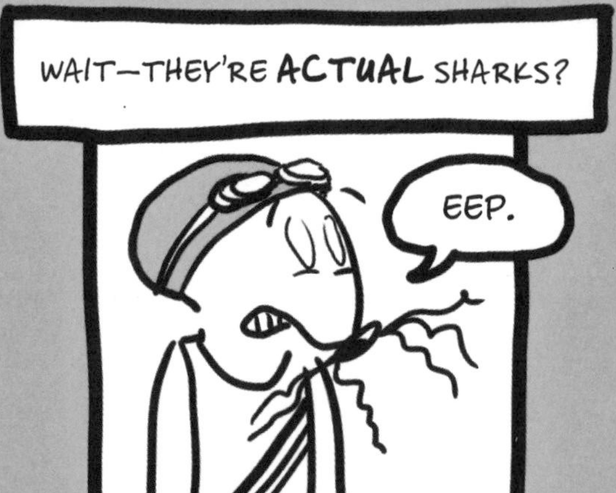
WAIT—THEY'RE ACTUAL SHARKS?
EEP.

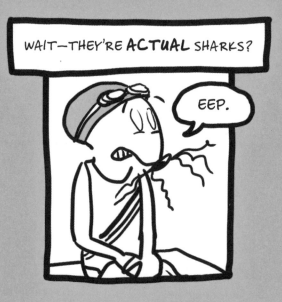

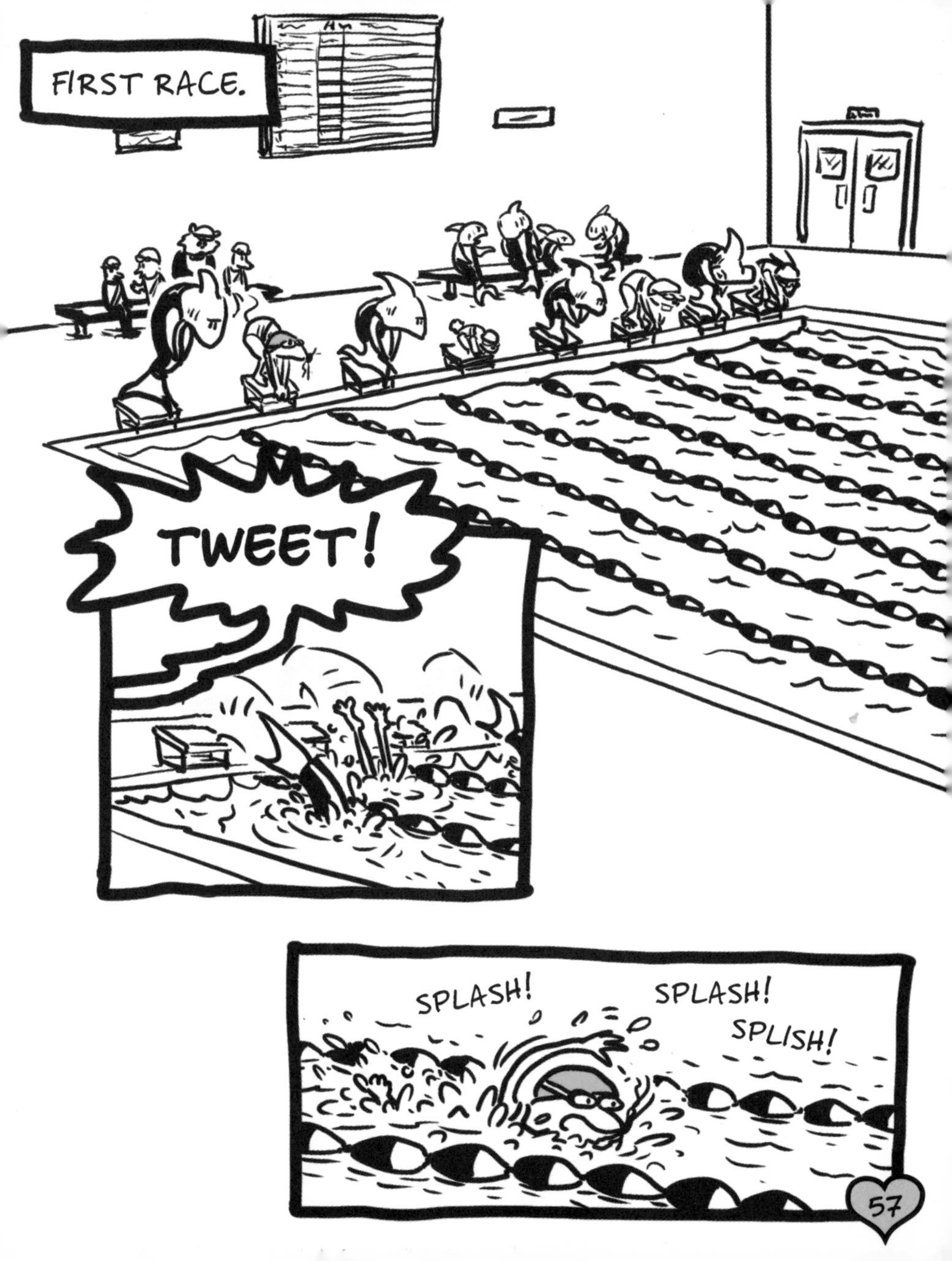
FIRST RACE.
TWEET!
SPLASH!
SPLASH!
SPLISH!

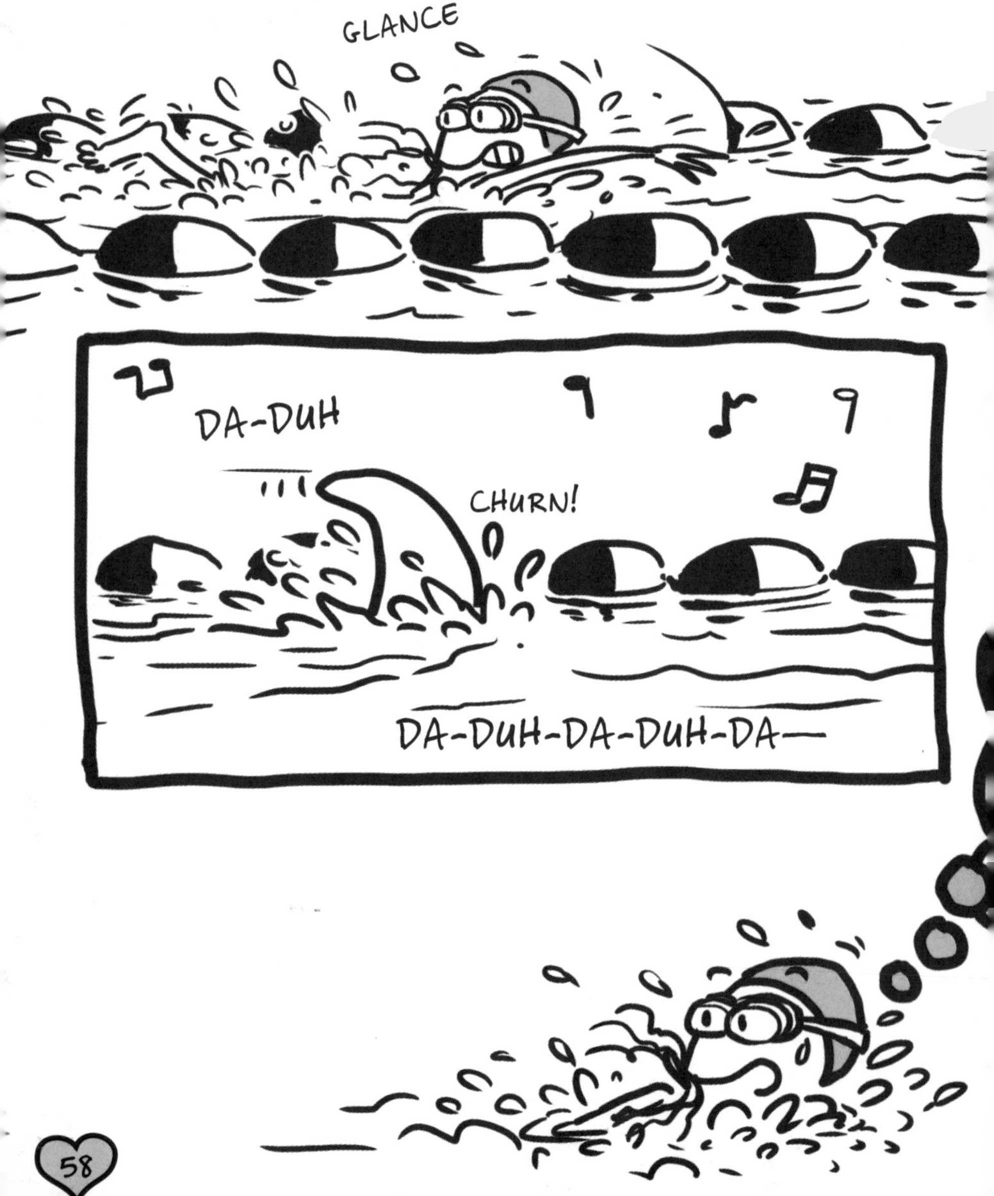
GLANCE
DA-DUH
CHURN!
DA-DUH-DA-DUH-DA—

TUG!

BLOOP!

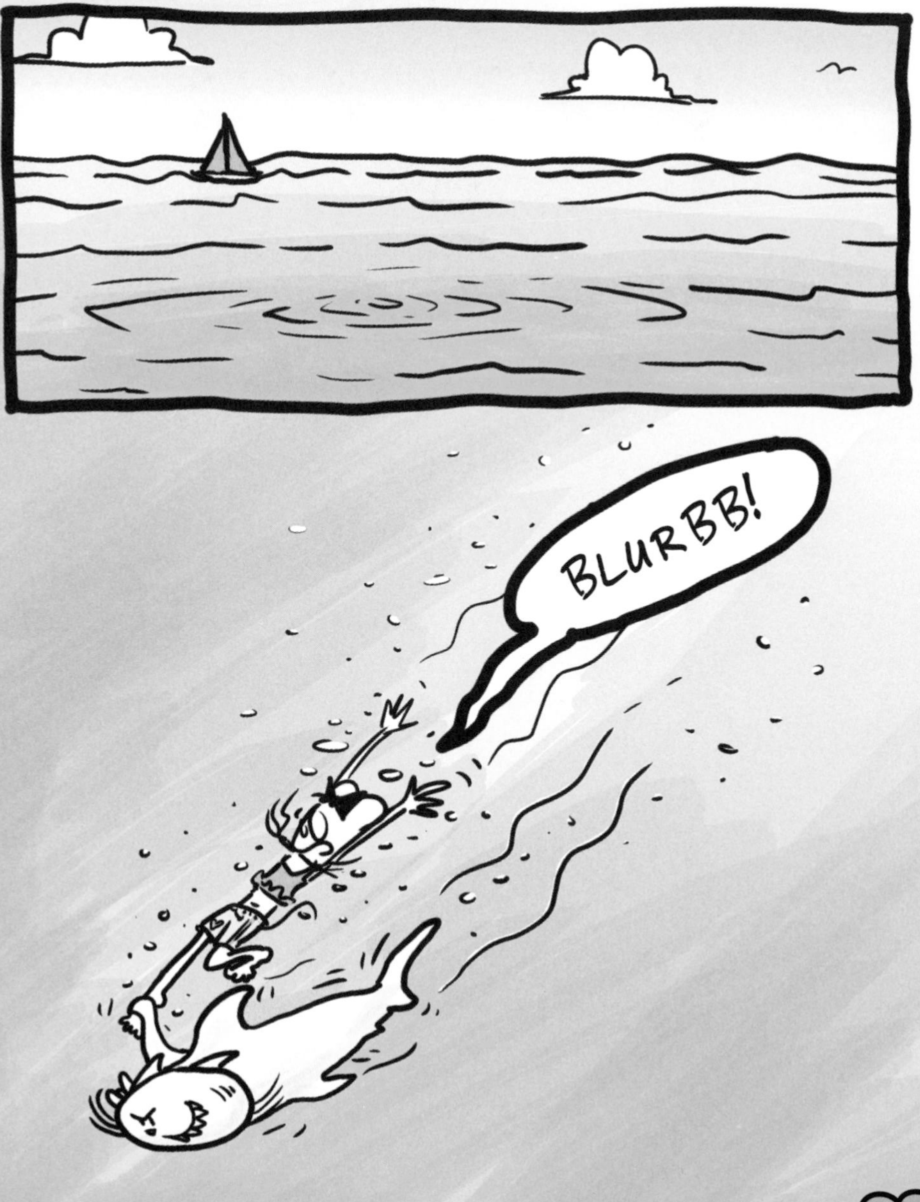
BLURBB!

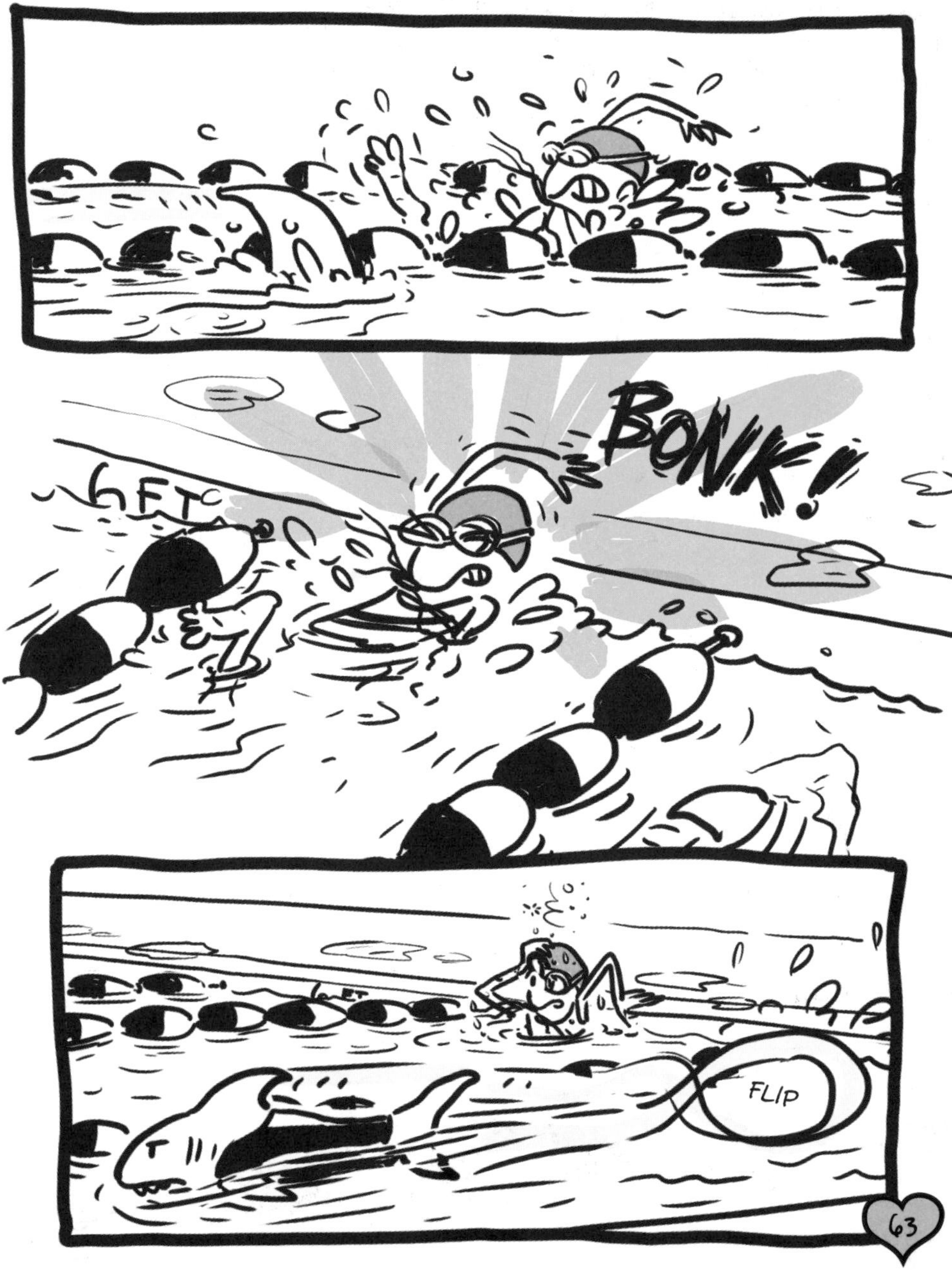
6FT
BONK!
FLIP

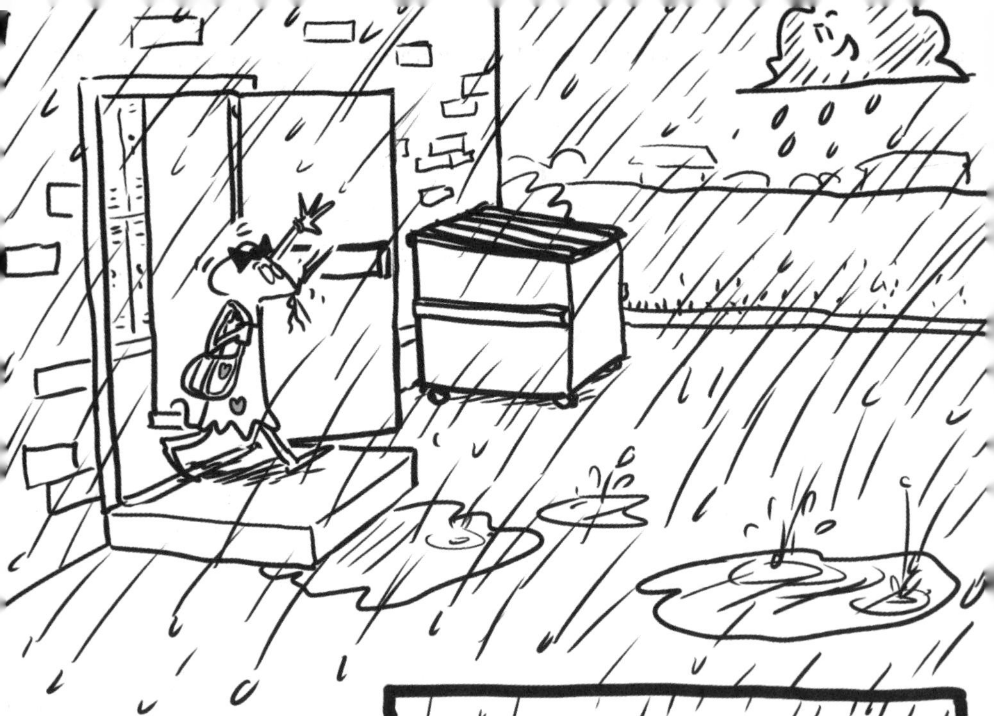

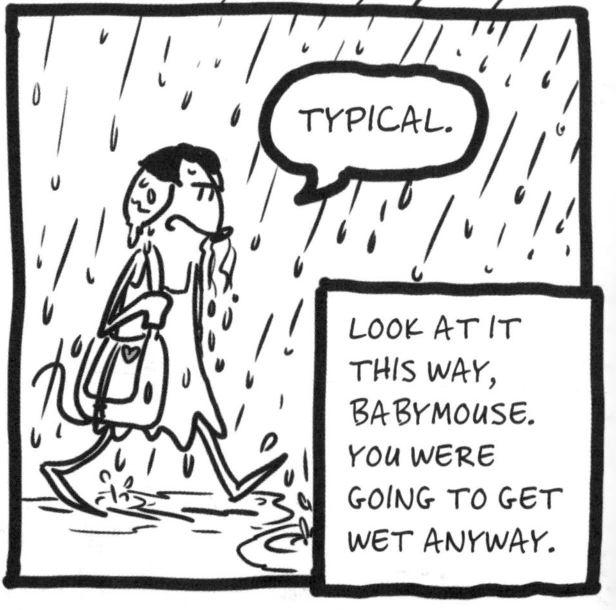
TYPICAL.
LOOK AT IT THIS WAY, BABYMOUSE. YOU WERE GOING TO GET WET ANYWAY.

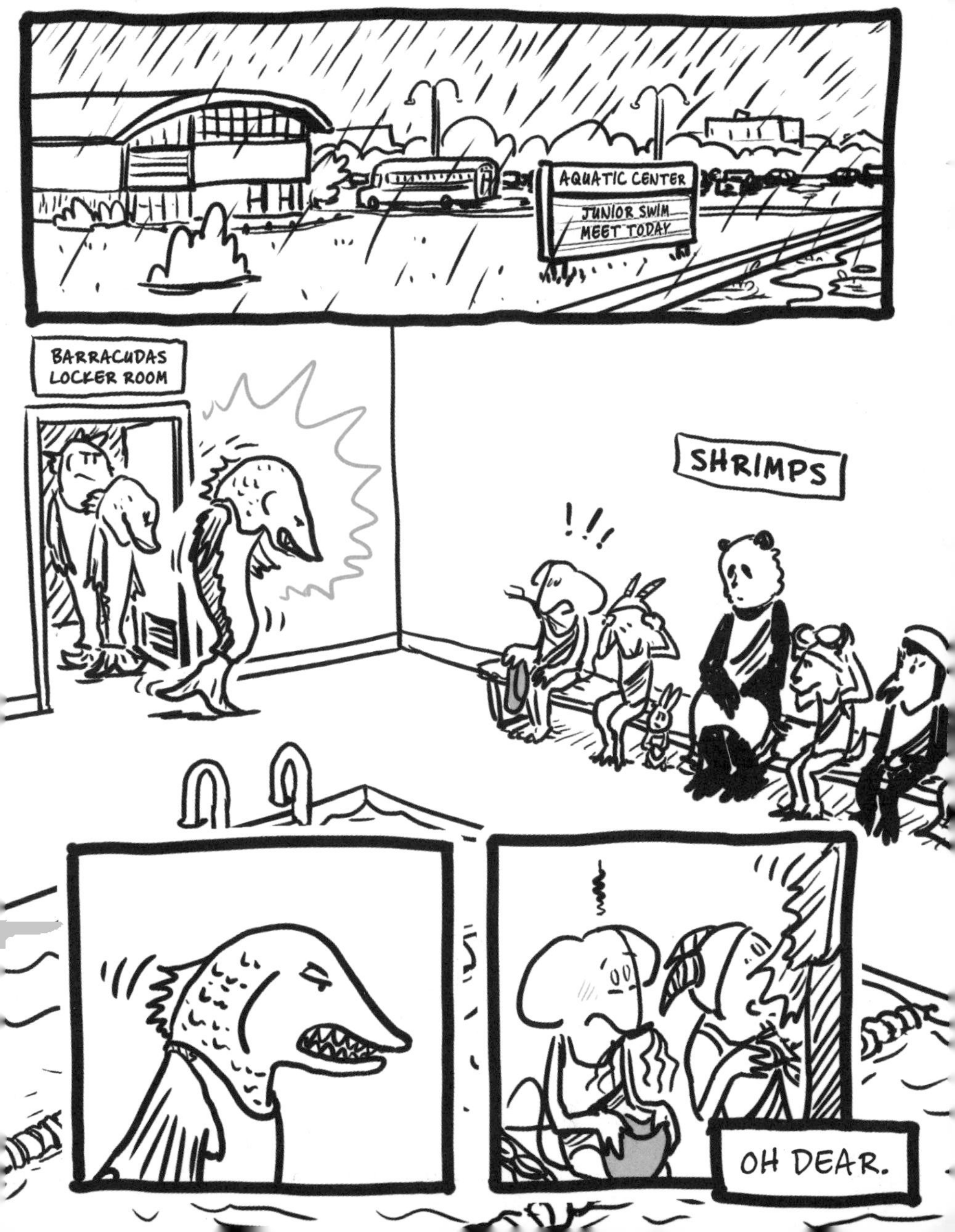
AQUATIC CENTER
JUNIOR SWIM MEET TODAY
BARRACUDAS LOCKER ROOM
SHRIMPS
!!!
OH DEAR.

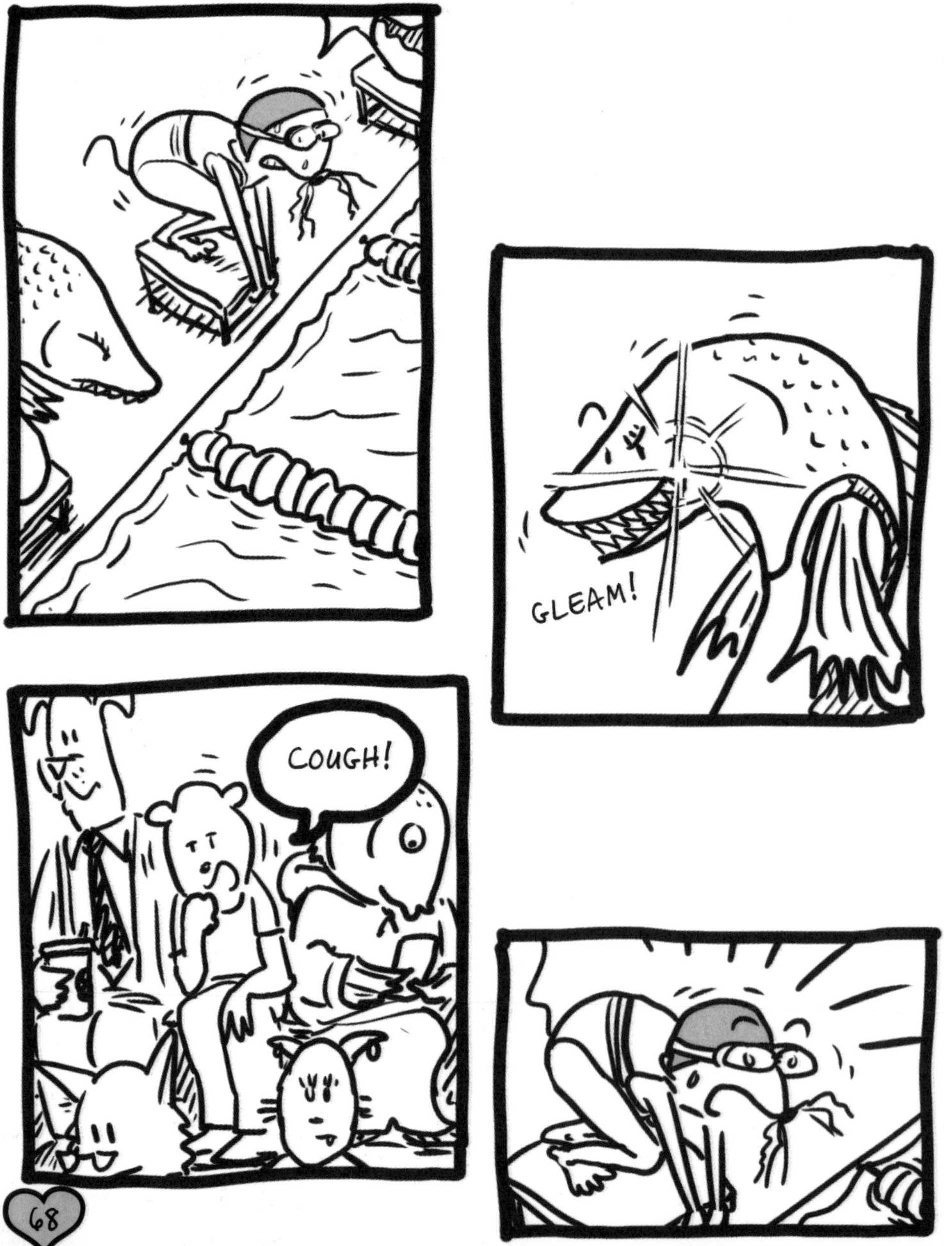
GLEAM!
COUGH!

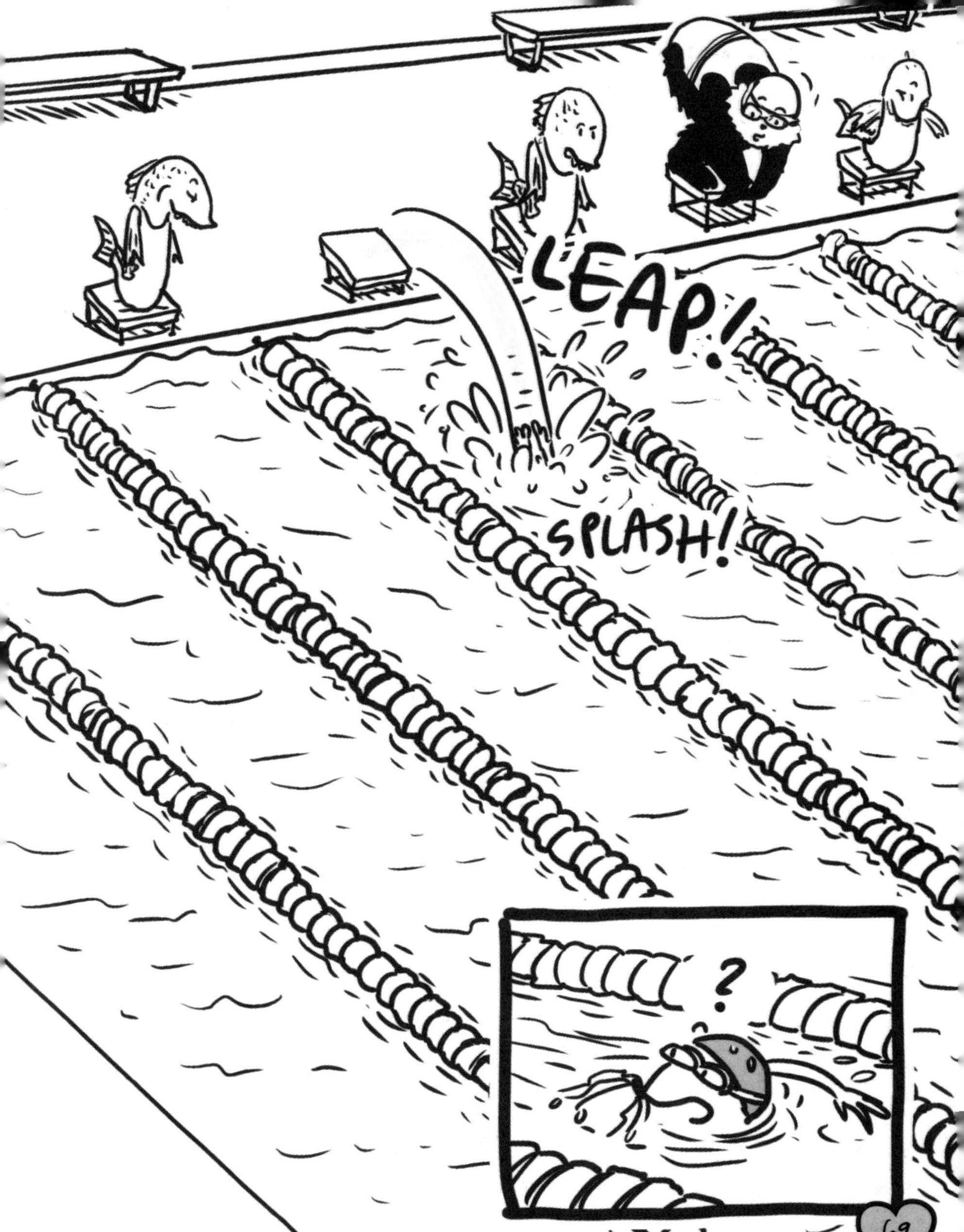
LEAP!
SPLASH!
?

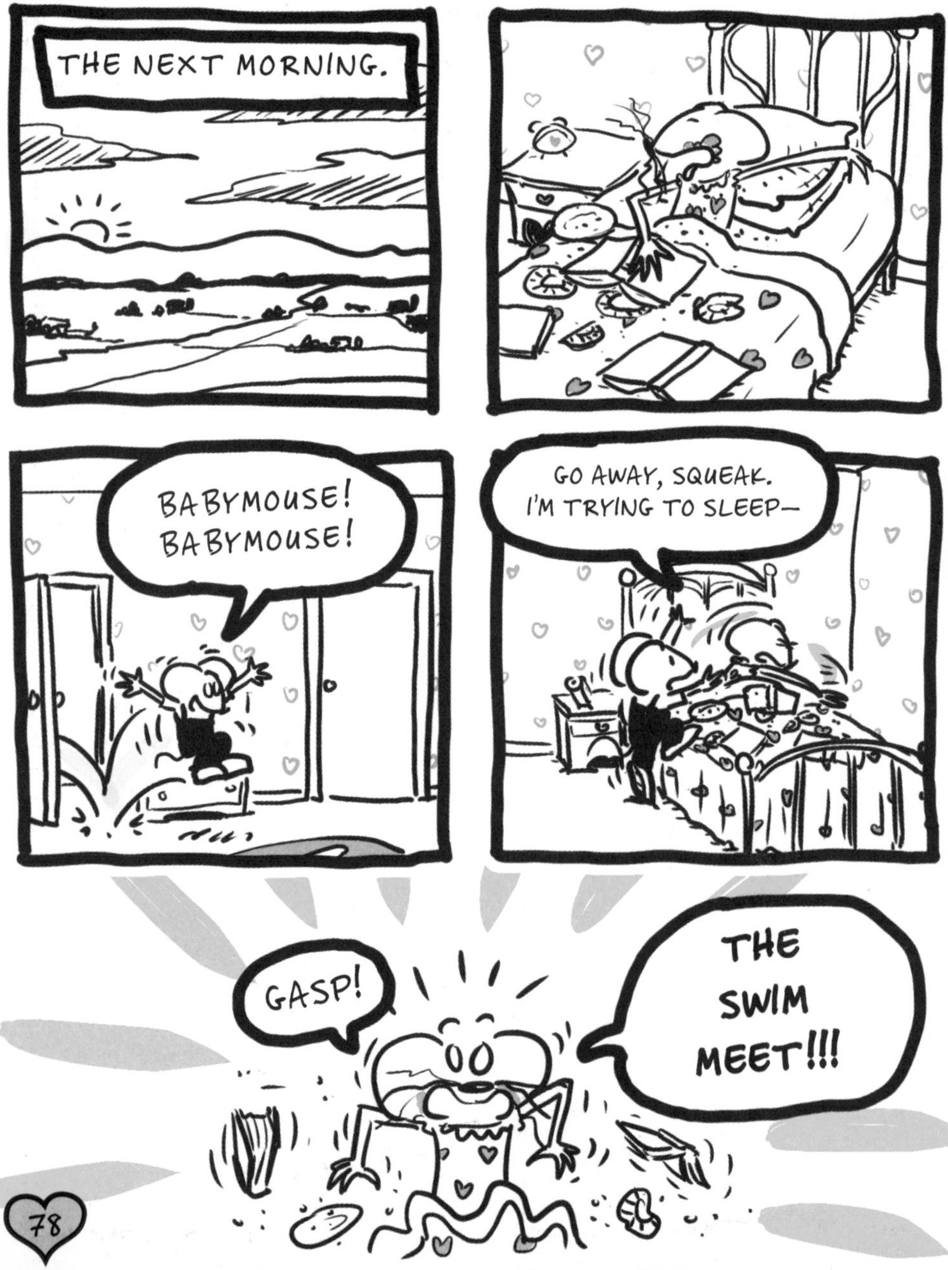
THE NEXT MORNING.
BABYMOUSE! BABYMOUSE!
GO AWAY, SQUEAK. I'M TRYING TO SLEEP—
GASP!
THE SWIM MEET!!!

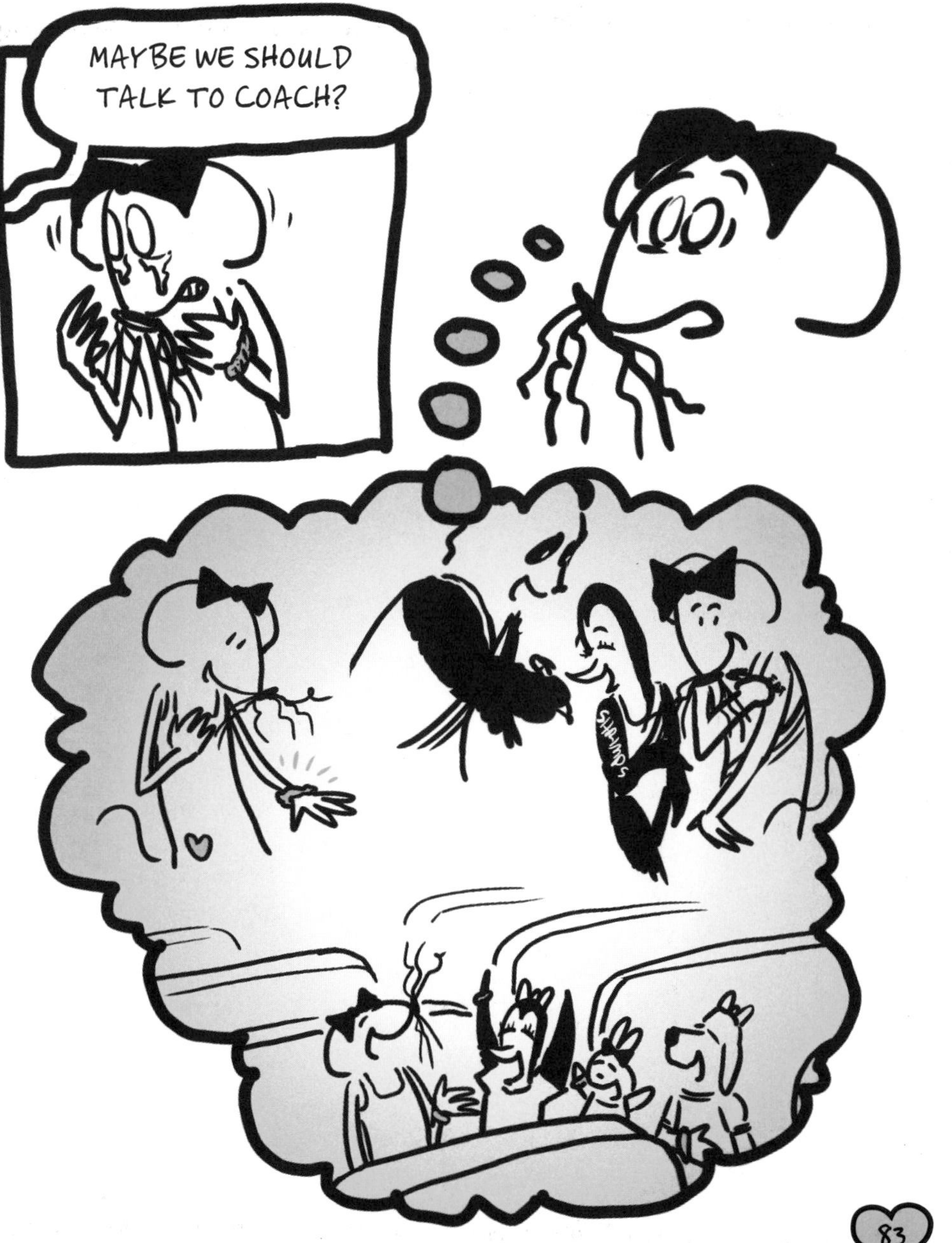
MAYBE WE SHOULD TALK TO COACH?

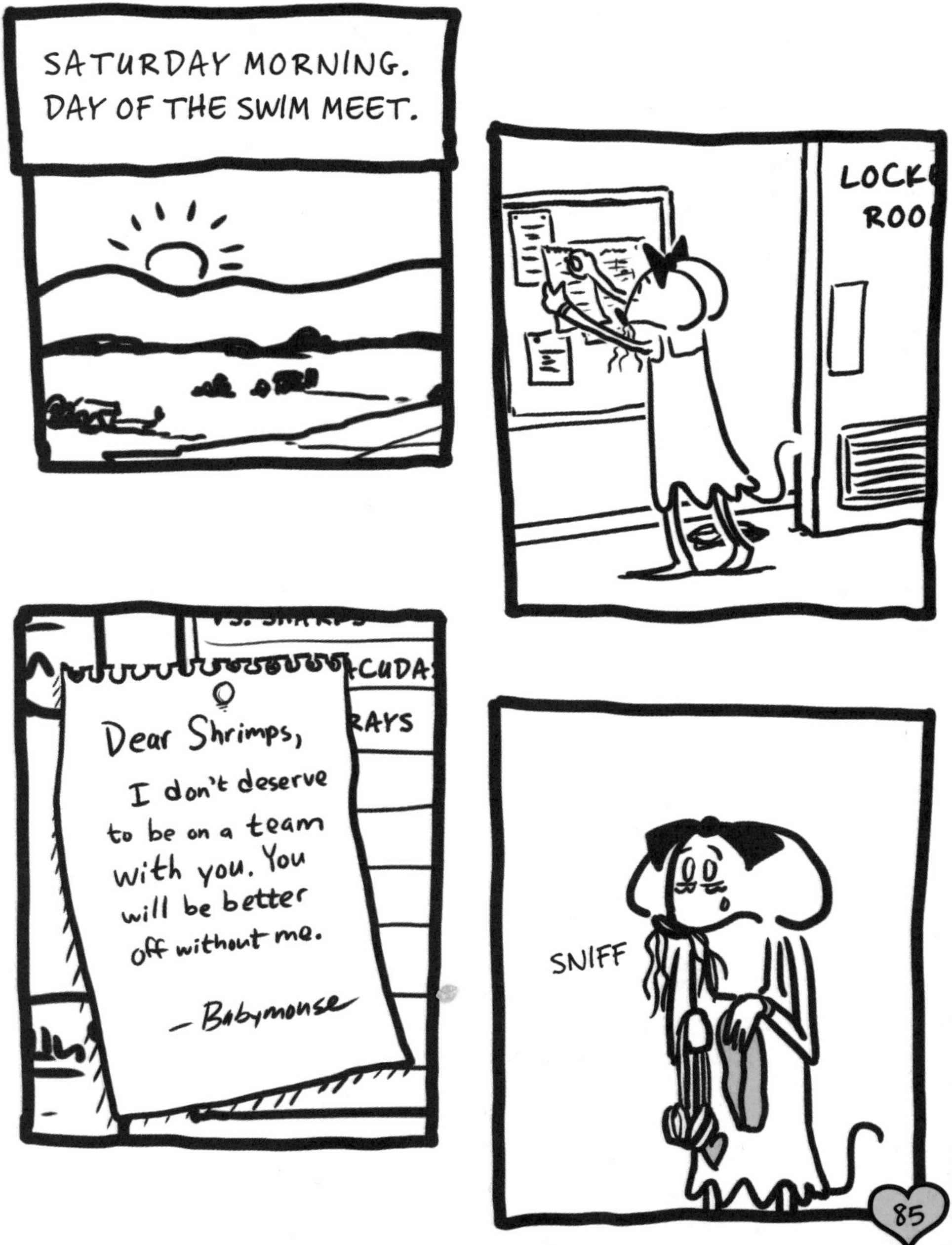
SATURDAY MORNING.
DAY OF THE SWIM MEET.
Dear Shrimps,
I don't deserve to be on a team with you. You will be better off without me.
— Babymouse
SNIFF

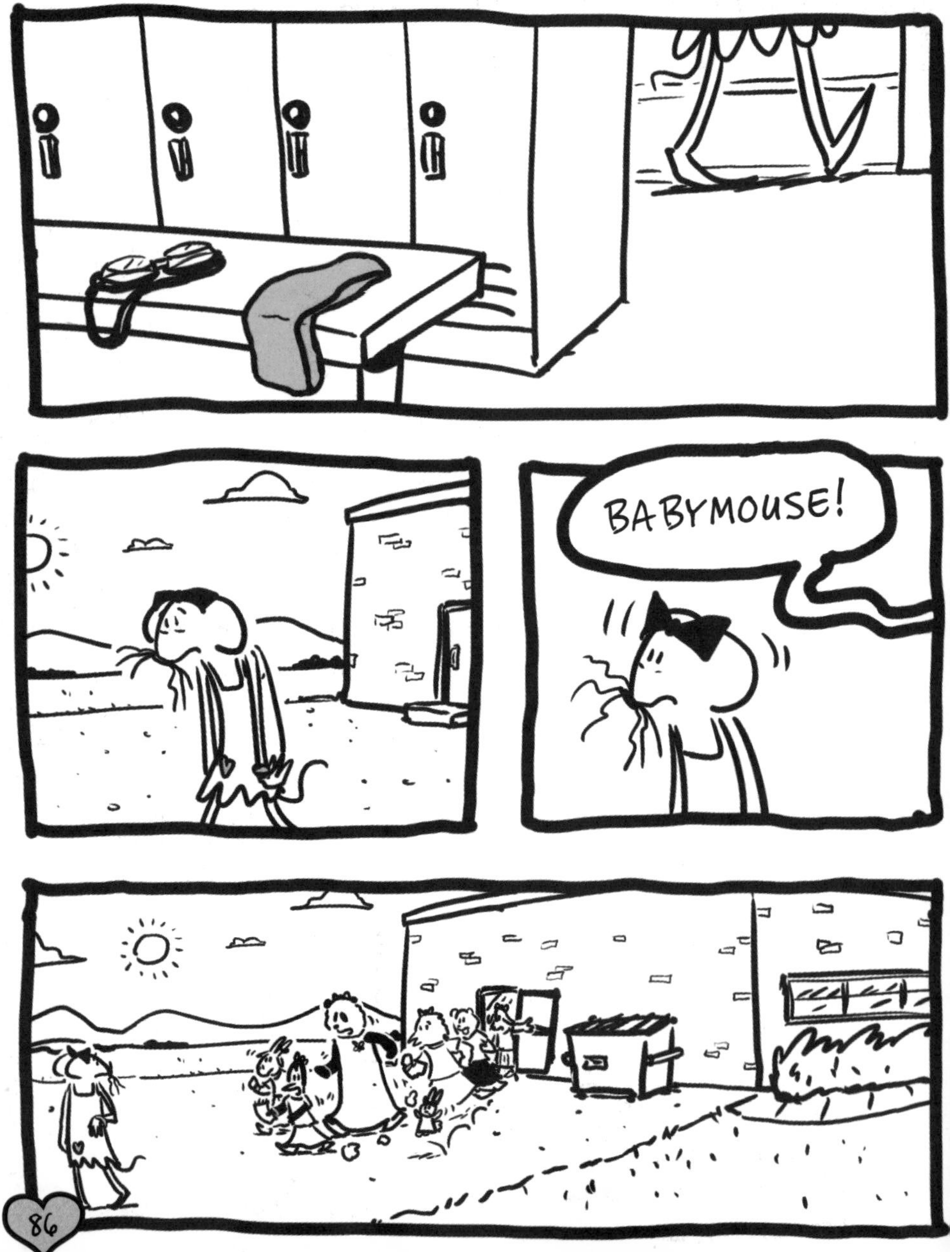
BABYMOUSE!

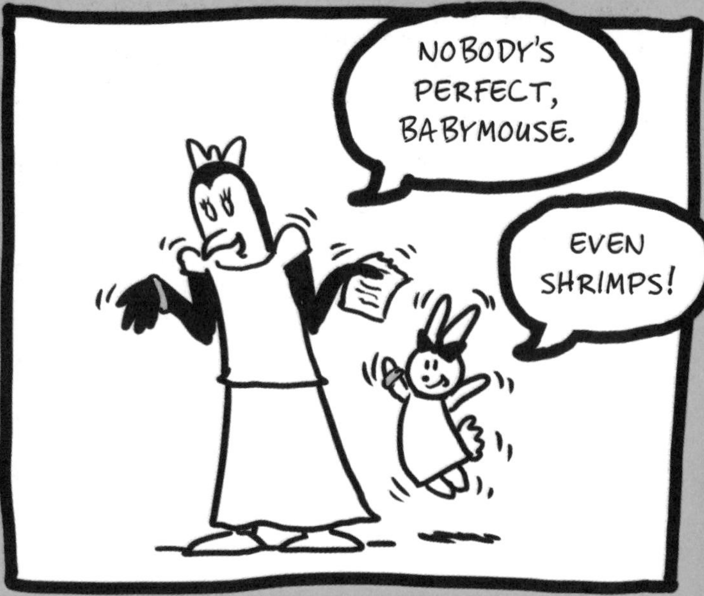
NOBODY'S PERFECT, BABYMOUSE.
EVEN SHRIMPS!

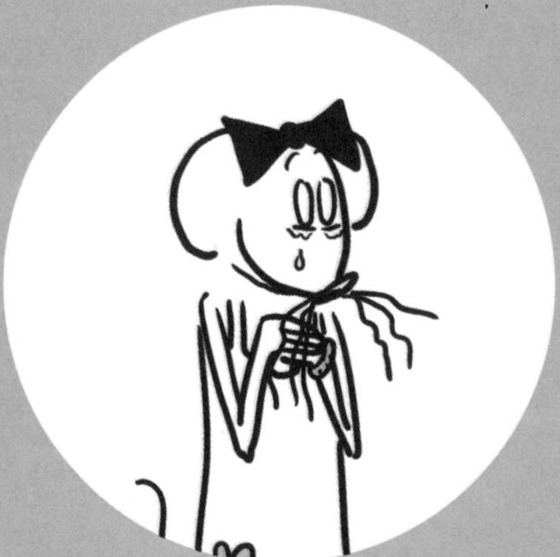

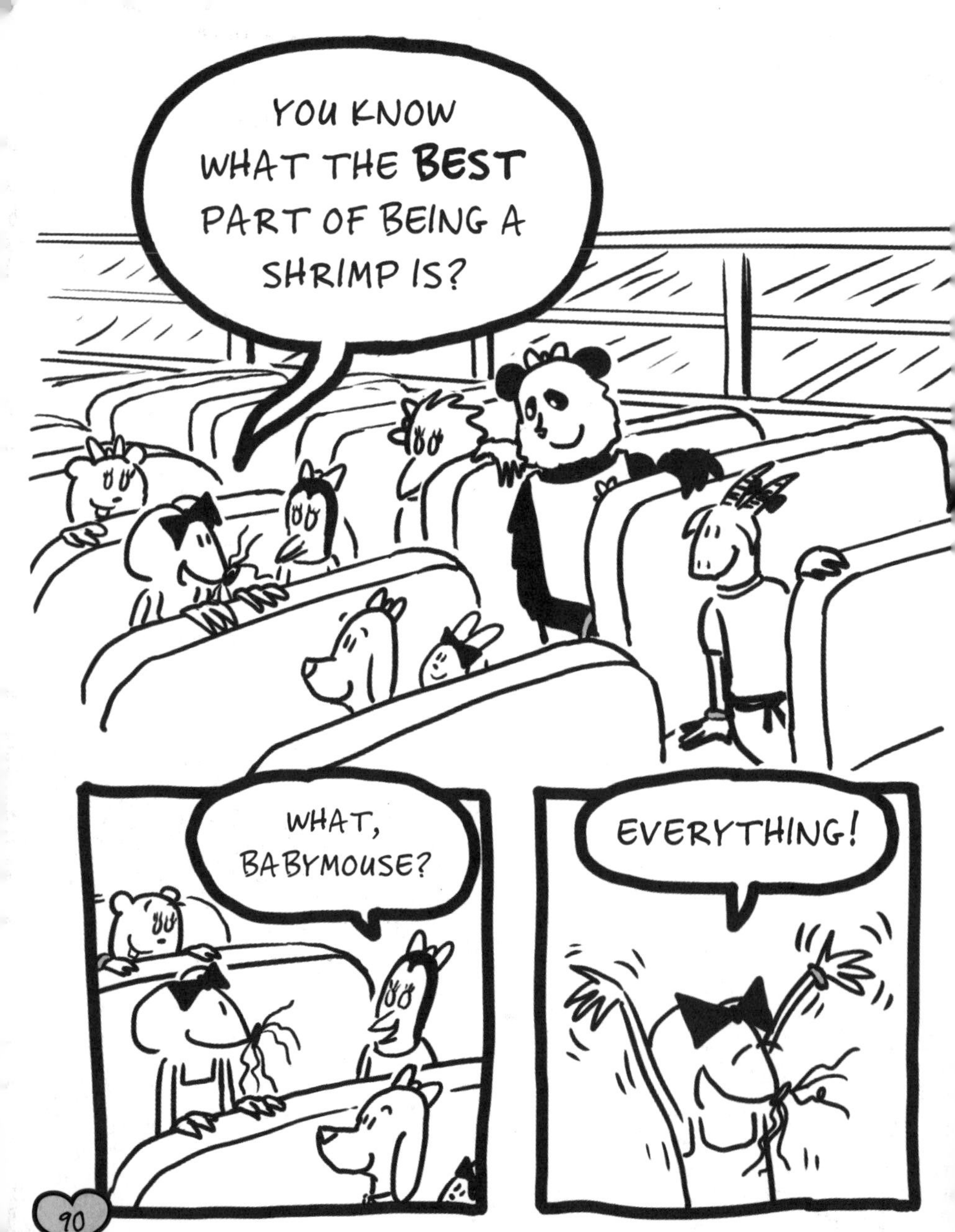
YOU KNOW WHAT THE **BEST** PART OF BEING A SHRIMP IS?
WHAT, BABYMOUSE?
EVERYTHING!

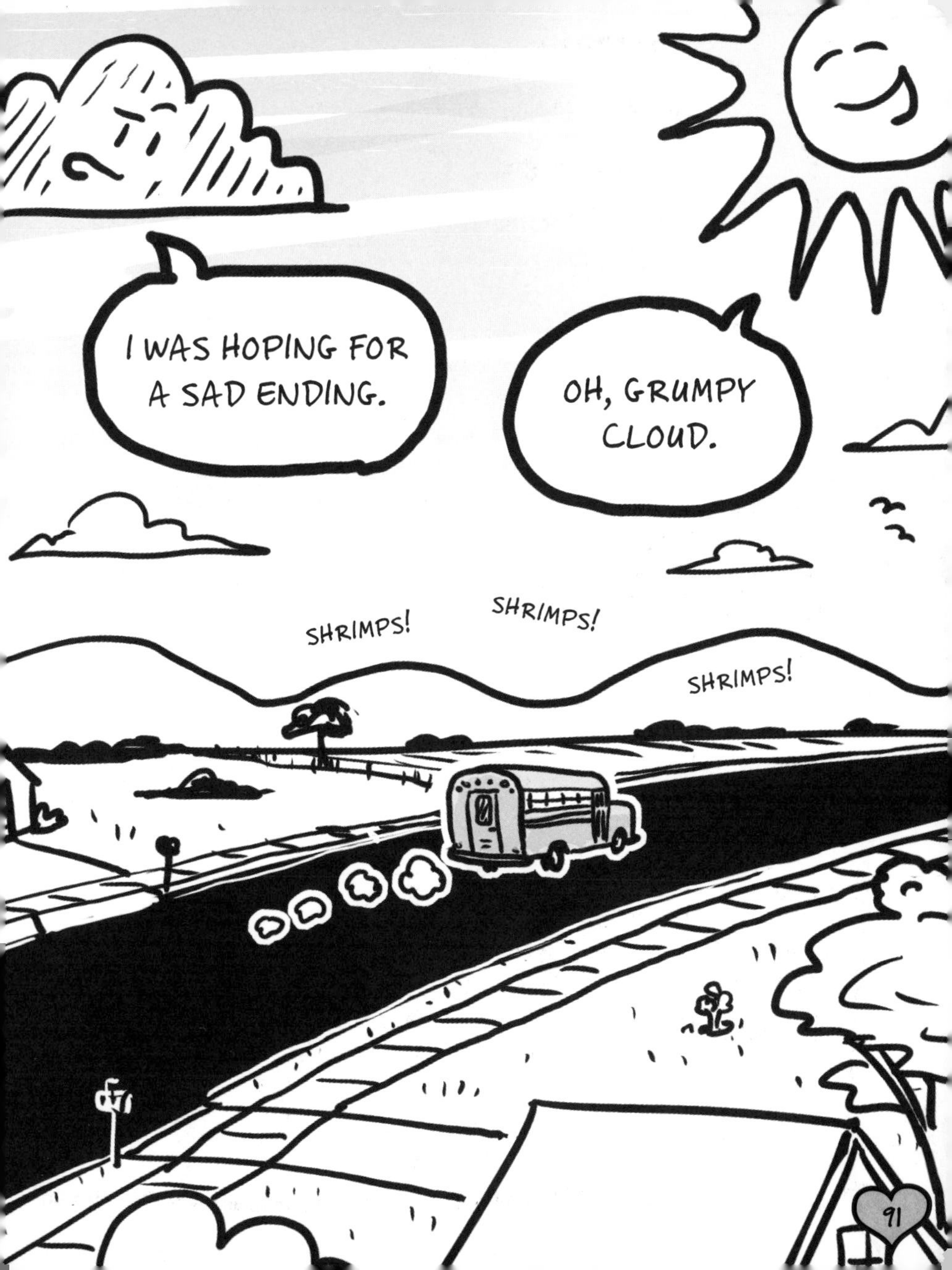
I WAS HOPING FOR A SAD ENDING.
OH, GRUMPY CLOUD.
SHRIMPS!
SHRIMPS!
SHRIMPS!

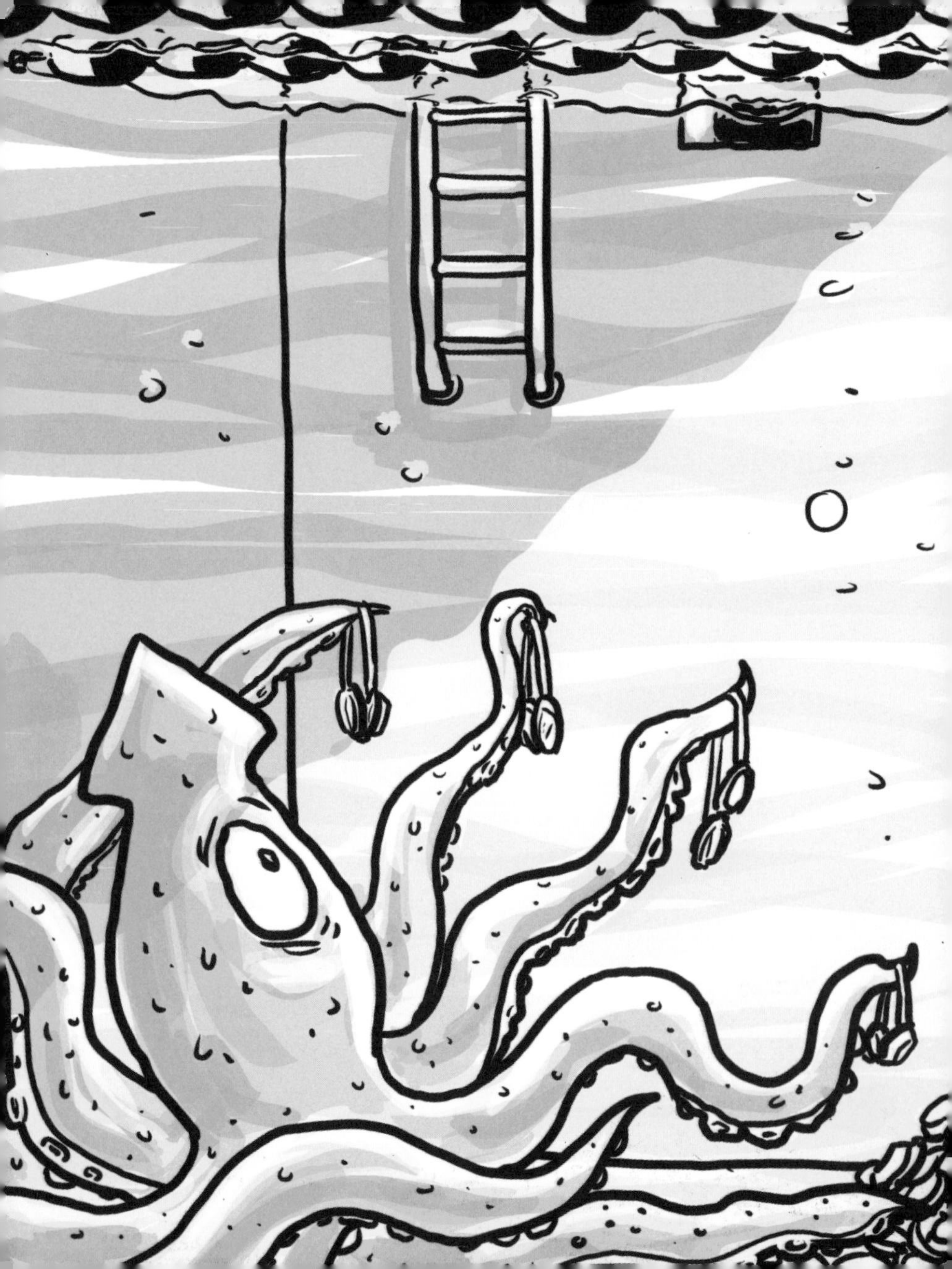

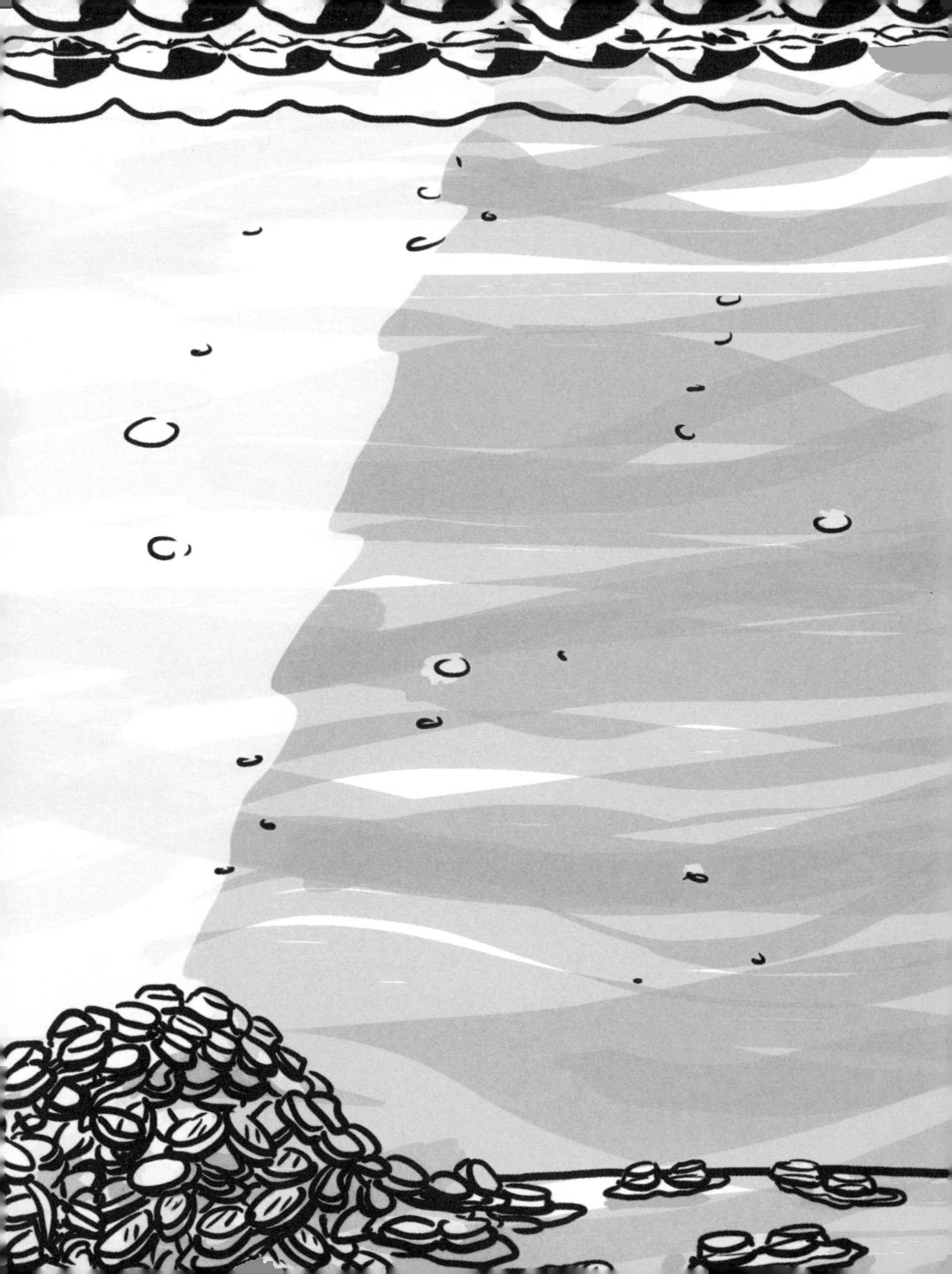

READ ABOUT
SQUISH'S AMAZING ADVENTURES IN: